THE TOUCH OF BREEZE

PRITILATA NANDI

Contents

Contents

In loving memory of my late husband, Sri Arunangshu Nandi, and with deep respect for my dear mother-in-law, Smt. Gita Nandi, I dedicate this book. Their unwavering love, support, and inspiration have guided me throughout my journey, and it is in their cherished memory that these words find their place. May their spirits forever shine upon these pages, filling them with the warmth and wisdom they brought into my life.

Foreword

Welcome to a captivating world woven by Pritilata, a remarkable woman who wears the hats of a math teacher, mother, and devoted writer. Within these pages, she shares her imaginative stories, transporting you to realms of wonder and emotions. As you delve into the tapestry of her characters and places, remember that every element is born solely from her creative brilliance. While coincidences may surface, all portrayed here is purely fictional. Pritilata's tales capture the joys and sorrows of ordinary women, showcasing their strength and resilience. Embrace the boundless potential of her imagination, as you discover the beauty in the seemingly ordinary. May this book inspire you, leaving you with a renewed love for storytelling and the indomitable spirit of a passionate woman.

- Pritilata Nandi

Preface

Welcome to a realm of emotions and boundless imagination, brought to life by the extraordinary talent of Pritilata Nandi, the creative mind behind this book. Within these pages lies a beautifully woven love story that is sure to resonate with the depths of your heart.

Pritilata's words possess a rare simplicity that holds immense power, making this tale accessible to all readers, yet profound enough to leave a lasting impact.

This book is a celebration of love and the art of storytelling, where ordinary moments are transformed into extraordinary encounters, and the characters' emotions dance off the page. As you journey through this enchanting narrative, you will find yourself captivated by the profound connection between the protagonist and the essence of human experience.

To all those who embark on this literary voyage, I extend my heartfelt gratitude. May this story kindle a spark in your hearts, allowing you to reflect on the beauty of love and the resilience of the human spirit.

With warm wishes for your happiness and well-being, I hope you enjoy this magical odyssey penned by Pritilata Nandi.

Acknowledgements

Gratitude fills my heart as I acknowledge the pivotal influences that shaped my writing journey. To my daughter, Arundhati Nandi, thank you for introducing me to the world of writing and igniting my passion for storytelling.

My deepest appreciation goes to the blogging community on WordPress, and to the blogger followers who have joined me on this creative odyssey. Your support and encouragement have been my driving force.

Sougata Mazumder, your unwavering assistance has been a guiding light throughout this process, and I am sincerely grateful for your contributions. And I am very much thankful to my friend Kirankumar Aher for the cover photo.

A special thanks to my brother, Ashish Kumar, for believing in me and making this book's publication a reality.

To all those who have touched my life and inspired me, thank you for being a part of this incredible journey.

CHAPTER ONE

THE TOUCH OF BREEZE

THE TOUCH OF BREEZE(PART-1)

After a long time,65 years old Susmita packed her Saree and dresses for a tour of Harshil , Gangotree. When Arijit was alive they visited most of the famous places of India. Though Arijit planned this tour many times,it didn't happen then. Her only son Ashis forced her to go with them during the Puja holidays.

Her only granddaughter, Silpa, helped her to pack her stuff. She was very excited that ultimately they got Susmita to agree to go with them. She hugged her and said,'' Granny, you know I am very happy. Dad has booked two rooms in the hotel. One is for Mom and Dad. And another is for us. At night we will talk there. I want to listen to your teenage love story. You know my friends always say,' Your Granny is an excellent woman. If we have such a wonderful Granny like you then we will feel lucky". And I feel so proud of you". Susmita laughed and adored her by touching her cheeks," Oh ho! That's it! I thought I would listen to your special person from you. What do you think? I don't know anything. I saw you talk over the phone secretly ".

Silpa felt shy and kept her fo finger on Susmita's lips and said,'' Granny ,stop! Stop! Don't speak loudly. Mom is coming. If she listens to all. You don't know what will happen. Granny ,you promised me you will tell your love story except with Dadan(Shilpa calls Arijit, Dadan means grandpa) "

In the meantime,Rina came. Seeing her they both stopped. Rina said," Silpa, after finishing Granny's packing. Make your luggage.

Take everything that you need. And don't ask me for anything there. Remember it." Sipa said ," Mom, don't worry I will do everything."

At noon they reached Howra station. Their train was Kumbha Express.They would come back by flight via Dehradun. There they will stay at Rina's aunt's house. Ashish wanted to do both in flight but Susmita wanted to feel the essence of journey by train when she went with Arijit.

In the first class, AC Susmita took the lower berth. At night everyone got asleep but she couldn't close her eyes. It was her usual problem. If she changes her bed she can't sleep easily.It takes time. Lots of past memories of her life came to her mind.She sank into it. Susmita was a school teacher by profession. Now she is a famous writer. One of her books was picturized in a Hindi movie and it became superhit.

After graduation her parents got her married to Arijit. It was an arranged marriage. He was ten years older than Susmita. At that time her dad Subas was not financially sound. Susmita had a little brother also. She was not fair. Her parents were looking for a groom for Susmita. One day Arijit came to see Susmita with one of the known persons of Subas. He liked her at first sight. After talking to her Arijit told Subas," If you agree then I don't have any problem marrying her. I have only my mom. My dad is no more. My only sister is married and she lives in Delhi. My decision is final. Before fixing anything my mom and my relatives will come to meet Susmita ".

So after a few days Arijit's family members came to visit Susmita. Arijit's mom Nipa liked her very much. So within one month, their marriage was fixed. He was very good looking and had no demand. So they didn't try to check anything about his work or nature.

Susmita started her married life with love for Arijit. Because before him she didn't get in touch with any man so intimately and for the first time Arijit gave her the taste of traveling. She never went on any tour before marriage. Her dad had not the financial condition to avail that.

After marriage Arijit wanted to know where she would like to go in honeymoon? She wanted to see the sea. So they went to Digha. That was her first outing.

After marriage Susmita used to know that Arijit worked in a central government office as a casual fourth class staff with little salary. He had one month off and one month had to go to the office. And he didn't like his work as a fourth-class staff in the office. He got the job in his dad's office after his sudden death. He couldn't finish his graduation.

On the off day, he spent most of his time sleeping. He was very lazy. His mom did all the duties, like grocery shopping etc. She was a pension holder. So financially she also took all the responsibilities. If Susmita or Nipa said to Arijit for any household work he answered, " I was not born to do all the silly things".

Susmita was very surprised to see it all. She saw her dad as a hard-working and responsible person. A Bengali woman likes to get a husband like her dad. Most of his office days he didn't want to go to the office. Susmita didn't like it. If she forced him to go to work and he got angry. He had three passionate job sleeping without tension, taking medicines and going out of station .Whatever he earned he saved for traveling.

On the other hand, Susmita got pregnant within two months of marriage. Though she didn't want to become a mom so early. But it happened. Arijit wanted it very much so he bought vitamin pills instead of contraceptive pills and gave it to her. She didn't have any doubt and took them daily. When she got to know she wanted to have an abortion but her mom-in-law Nipa said, "Susmita don't abort, please. This is your first child. Let the new life come. You don't need to think at all. I will take care of the baby like my child. After your dad-in-law is gone I am so lonely. I need a friend for me. I beg you give it to me."

So after Ashish's birth, her Amma (Ashish called his granny as Amma) took all the responsibilities for him. She fed him, took care of him , and always gave company to him. All said," Nipa has become a new mom." And she laughed a lot hearing it. She replied," Yes, yes Ashish is not only my grandson but a new blessing for my life like his name's meaning (Ashish means blessing). And I want to live for him. I believe that Arijit's dad came as Ashish".

After giving birth to her son Susmita realized she had to do something. Because only a little pension from Nipa was not enough for the family. Sometimes Arijit became very violent towards his mom. Very often They argued with each other by closing the door. One day she saw Arijit slapping his mom. Then her son Ashish was one year old.

After that incident, she asked Arijit," Why did you slap your mom? Shame on you. Go and apologies now. I can't think of you as so bad! You showed us you are a great person and had a good family and now you are doing such a dirty thing."

Then Arijit told her," What do you know about me? Have you ever asked me why I like to sleep most of the time? I want to forget my past. Do you know I am a patient with depression for my mom. I have been taking antidepressant pills since the age of 22. How much I love my mom and that much I hate her."

" What are you saying? I never saw you taking medicine. Why didn't you say everything before our marriage?" Susmita shouted.

" I took medicine secretly at night when you remain busy cooking dinner. I didn't tell you because I wanted a companion and my spouse! Please forgive me. I will never forgive my parents for ruining my life." Arijit told.

" No! You and your mom did wrong with me! No relationship can stay on a lie. We are poor, I am dark and that's why you took that advantage. Don't you"? Susmita said.

Arijit tried to stop her by saying," Listen I was a very good student. I always stood first in class. I wanted to be a doctor. Then I was in class four. That time we left our grandfather's house and went to a rented house. My dad was a central government employee. When I was in class seven one day my dad said ' Don't need to be a doctor who kills people '. Within a few days, I will leave my job and will start a business with my friends. I met a talented young man whose name is T. Chakraborty (All called him Gurudev). He said to me if our company forms then we don't need to think about anything. He is our main owner. Then I have to remain busy in our business as a director. So finish your graduation with commerce then you will join there as a board of directors."

So after a few months, my dad started a company taking voluntary retirement from his job. We moved to a new flat in a lavish area .The company's name was 'Sanchayi' . It was a small savings or Ponzi scheme company.They collected money from common people promising to give a high rate of interest. The company invested that money to buy lands at a lower price then sold its high price. Within a few months the company began to flourish. They opened many branches throughout West Bengal. Slowly it became famous. Lots of people started joining as agents. They collected money mostly from the poor classes as representatives of the company. For almost five years the company gave high interest and gained people's trust. So more and more people started keeping their money for the long term. I was preparing myself to join the company. Now the real game has started. Few dishonest agents kept the collected money behind them instead of giving it to the company. This system got viral as the company did not have any system to stop this kind of stealing. My dad and other board members realized something wrong was happening.They alerted the Gurudev , T. Chakraborty lots of times. The main owner Gurudev was a great fraud. Then he was busy playing love with aged women (Like my mom). He was very young, handsome, and smart. And he spoke beautifully. So women fall in love with him easily. He liked to stay around women. The women tried to make him happy and they became jealous of each other. My dad tried to tell him to take some steps against this kind of stealing. He didn't pay any attention.Then he was busy having a romance with my mom and other beautiful wives of the board of directors. In the afternoon my sister and I went to school and dad stayed at Sanchay's office. Then he came and slept with my mom. One afternoon I came from school a little earlier for some reason and I caught my mom and the gurudev having a romance on my mom's bed .I cried a lot. I didn't believe how my mom cheated on my dad. I kept it hidden in my soul. I love my mom very much.From that day a hatred came to my mind for the women. When I was in the first year of graduation the company was going down. My dad told me to start something with studying instead of joining the company. So I opened a printing office with one of my friends Rajat. We collected orders from the client's and made the design as per their wish and then printed them in big press and supplied them.It was running well. Suddenly Rajat got a job. After his leaving I couldn't run it well alone. On the other hand, my dad's company closed as they didn't return money to the people. So many agents were arrested. Police caught all the board of directors including my dad. My mom sold most of her jewelry to proceed with the case in court. She appointed one of the famous lawyers. After one year my dad got free.T. Chakraborty got a long punishment of six years in prison. During this time we became poor. We went for a normal rented house. My sister and I couldn't finish our study. I couldn't take all the mess. My friends laughed at me saying,'A thief's son'. My mom begged for money from our relatives to run our family. My dad started tuition by going home to home." While saying all Arijit's eyes filled with tears.Susmita asked," What happened to your printing business?"

Arijit answered," Then my office was the only place of happiness for me. We appointed a receptionist there. She was Mahua. She was a very fair and cute girl. She could play guitar well. We liked each other very much . So one day I proposed to her and she accepted it.We dreamed of a beautiful life together. We thought about getting married. On Sundays we watched movies, enjoyed food from restaurants, and roamed Kolkata by catching each other's hands. How many nights I imagined her as my wife! One of her birthdays I gave her a beautiful pink saree. And the next day she came to the office wearing it. She was looking so gorgeous I could not move my eyes from her. That day first I kissed on her forehead. She felt so shy .But after the disaster at my dad's company everything changed. We got separated".

" I am so sorry for that. If you love each other then why didn't you stop her?" Susmita asked.

Arijit told," I tried to stop her from my heart. She was scared about the future. She loved me very much. She wanted a secure life.That time it was impossible.One of my paternal aunt Phulu Pisi was her relative. She poisoned her and her family against us. She was jealous of us. My aunt couldn't tolerate our sudden prosperity. But I thought I could manage Mahua by making her understand my situations. She didn't come to the office for a few days". "Then what happened? " Susmita asked.

CHAPTER TWO

THE TOUCH OF BREEZE

THE TOUCH OF BREEZE(PART:2)

After one week Mahua came to my office with tears and said,"Arijit , I am so sorry I can't continue this relationship further. My family docs not agree with my decisions. My dad requested me not to make mistakes in life. I can't put down my parents in front of all. So goodbye. Stay happy. Forgive me if I hurt you.I am also leaving my job."

I begged her not to leave me alone. But she didn't listen.I will never forgive Phulu Pisi". Arijit said.

Susmita could still memorize all the words of Arijit of that day. He was looking so helpless. He was relaxed by saying everything to Susmita.

He continued,"Mahua left me. Rajat left the printing office. So I lost all the interest in my office. I felt so sad while going there.And within one year my office got closed. My dad didn't want to understand my problems. He always blamed me. My mom always supported me. After one year my dad's government office wanted new employees and gave advertisements in the newspaper. I applied and stood second in the test but unfortunately, the panel got canceled. One of the central ministers said it was unfair because only the employee's sons got a chance there. So they proposed a rule to cancel the advertisement. Twenty young people got a chance. Some of them went to court. My dad arranged for my beautiful sister's marriage in Delhi with the help of relatives with a very common guy who was fourteen years older than her. I protested hard but he didn't listen. All created pressure on me. After a few days I stopped going outside and talking to friends and I didn't want to eat either. Nothing felt good to me. I stayed alone,closing the door. I cried all the time. Dad scolded me for staying at home without work. My little aunt Mita's husband was a doctor that stupid said I needed vitamins. I was not getting well. My mom took me to another doctor. He suggested that I needed a phyciatrist. After counseling me the psychiatrist told me that I was going through deep depression and Ocd(Obsessive Compulsive Disorder).! He gave me lots of medicine. I slept the whole day. I always felt dizzy.Sometimes I became violent. My dad always said I was acting and nothing happened to me. Slowly I was getting well but I never became a jolly boy like earlier. The doctor said,' You would never leave these medicines throughout your life. Only the group will change according to the situation . Keep it in mind these pills are your dictator of life.' A good and healthy young man became a slave of medicines.Can you imagine Susmita ,how pathetic it is?"

"You didn't try to do something "? Susmita asked. "Yes, after feeling a little bit better I tried for a job. I couldn't finish my graduation so it was tough to get a good job. I was smart and good looking so I got a few jobs. Not so well. I felt bored after a few days . So after leaving that I joined a new one. My dad did not like it.If dad said sometime I got very angry with him. I thought that his wrong decision was responsible for all the mess in our lives. One day when I left one job and said it to home. My dad shouted at me and said, "You are a worthless boy. You will never do anything. See other boys at your age. What are they doing?Don't you feel ashamed to see your dad working so hard to manage everything? At this age I started tuition.And a pricey man like you! Leaving your job , sleeping the whole day."

" I got furious that night. First time I argued with my dad so hard. I roared," You are responsible for the disaster. You are a stupid man.Your all decisions were wrong from the very first day." My mom tried to stop me but I didn't listen. I continued. "On the day you took us apart in a rented house from our Granny, that was the start of your mistake. Granny cried a lot. She requested you a lot. But you didn't listen. If you don't get apart you will not meet that Bhanda guru who ruined all our happiness in life".

Dad cried out," What will I do? It was not possible to stay at that home. I argued with my dad for a very small reason and he got a heart attack and he died. All blame came over me. I can't tolerate it.Your mom knows everything".

" I also know that. Granny told you not to hear anyone. You keep your persistence. Not only that, you left your secure government job and ran after an insecure life". I shouted.

"Oh what do you think? I did everything for myself? I wanted to make you happy.I thought it would make our life more comfortable. How can I know it will destroy our life? Who wants to harm myself? Giving birth to a son like you I have to regret". Dad said.

" My dream to be a doctor has finished.I became a mental patient. I couldn't finish my study. Everything finished only for you". I shouted.

My dad started howling and crying. My mom slapped me and said," Ari, stop my boy! now don't hurt your dad anymore".

Now all my anger went to my mom. I said," Why don't you stop dad? He never went to the psychiatrist with me. Never wanted to realize my sorrow. And now instead of telling him to stop ,you want me to stop? Hun , When I saw you and Bhandaguru on your bed I stopped myself. Did you forget it?" Saying all I understood I made a great mistake. My dad stared at my mom with a strange look. As if he couldn't believe it. We all were crying. I went to my room and closed the door and took two sleeping pills and fell asleep. I don't know what happened then. That night I didn't have my meal."

"The next day after waking up I saw my mom was cooking. I asked my mom" where is dad?" Mom said,"He went to do tuition". The next two days were normal. My dad stopped talking to me. After two days my dad left home in the morning and didn't come till afternoon. Generally he never did it. We didn't know where my dad was gone! We were looking for him everywhere. We went to the police and did a general diary. The next day we got the news of his suicide by drowning in a pool. All blamed me for my dad's death. As my dad was blamed for my grandfather's death.

After a few days my dad's office wanted to appoint a few boys who got a chance earlier . My mom went there and prayed for a job so they appointed me as fourth-class staff . I make tea there. I keep the files on the table. Do you think I deserve this? So I don't like my job". Arijit said.

Susmita said," I am so sorry for all. What is my fault? I dreamed about a beautiful life with my husband. I wanted a hard-working, responsible person in my life. But you are the opposite."

Arijit told,"Listen Susmita, I have not forced you to marry me. Why didn't your parents try to know everything about me? I am handsome , fair. You are dark. Then your dad should have to understand that maybe I have some fault. Why did they believe me blindly? Ask them. From today you know that I am like that. When I get angry I lose my sense. I can't control myself. Please Susmita, what happened! Now we can't change but I can say that me and my mom are happy to have you and Ashish in our family. I can't forget my past. I have to live with it."

Susmita said," Those are the past.You have to overcome everything. I don't know what to do? Only my tears are coming thinking about it all. What about the future of Ashish? I blame my luck".

Arijit tried to make her understand," I married you because I thought you were dark and from a poor family and as an educated woman you will understand me and adjust to everything. I thought you were soft."

Susmita answered ," I am a woman first. I have a heart like a fair woman. I feel jealous to see other happy couples. My mom and dad never quarreled. My dad still is doing all his duties. My mom never had to think about anything. But see me after my marriage every day I have to think about how to stay well ".

Arijit caught her hand and said," Because you are educated. You are not like your mom. Only men have to take all the responsibility!

Who said that? Hun! Time is changing now. What can I do? I don't feel good mentally. I can't show anyone my pain. It is not a physical illness.Those who have never suffered mental illness can't imagine how dangerous it is! Please Susmita try to understand. Yes, I did wrong not telling you about my illness for fear that you wouldn't agree to get married. I needed a companion and my spouse to fight against this boring life. My mom was very lonely before Ashish came. Now she always looks very happy. That gives me peace. I dream, though I did nothing for her but my son will make her proud. I indeed hate her but I love her madly for her strong mentality. She tried to save me till now she is doing that. You have to be like my mom. You have to protect us.We have no one except you , Susmita. Sometimes we don't have the option to deny our luck. I was in our fortune." Susmita remained stopped. She felt pain to see Arijit's situation. Whatever happened in her life, she forgot.That time Arijit was her priority. She started loving Arijit without knowing anything. She hugged Arijit and said," Let's dream to live a new life. But first I had to find a job". I will help you to find a job. Don't worry". Arijit said

Susmita started searching for a job. Arijit helped her a lot. One day Arijit took her to a big private school. Because getting a government job was tough. There they used to know that she has to take training about teaching. Susmita took admission in the course. She did well.She stood second .Then she applied as an English teacher and got the job. Then Ashish was two years old. Susmita was so happy. After coming home she touched Nipa's feet to take her blessings. Arijit hugged and kissed her and said," I knew you would do it. You are my brave wife. I had full faith in you."

Susmita thought life will be filled with happiness.Every morning she left for school. Nipa took great care of little Ashish and did a lot of things like making breakfast, cooking meals, giving bath to little Ashish. feeding him, and everything. She loved Susmita very much. Susmita also thought of her like own mom. In the evening Susmita looked after the kitchen but Nipa always helped her. In this way a beautiful adjustment formed in between them.

Susmita could remember after getting her first salary of Rs 750/ she bought a bermuda for Arijit, a beautiful set of dress for Ashish and a set of six glasses for Nipa.

Nipa said to her," Susmita , why didn't you bring something for you? Tomorrow you will certainly buy a saree for you". Susmita did that.Sometimes Arijit got very angry without any reason and shouted at home. In the meantime, Arijit left his casual job and started a business of supplying cold drinks with the partnership of his uncle's eldest son Srijit. His uncle helped them financially. Arijit was very hot-tempered. He got very intolerant with little things.Then most of the time he quarreled with Nipa and all the time he tried to taunt her by saying the name of Bhandaguru. This didn't make Susmita feel good. She felt very ashamed. Sometimes she protested against it. Then Arijit started arguing with her. The first few months their business was going well. Both of the cousin brothers worked hard. They took dealerships in a certain area. There they supplied the cold drinks shop to shop. And in the evening they collected money from those shops. They shared the profit between them equally. Susmita and Arijit both loved to tour. Though Arijit injected this passion to Susmita. It was only the common things in between them. So in the Summer vacation and Puja vacation at Susmita's school, they went out of the station with Ashish. Nipa did not like it either. But Arijit didn't listen to anyone about this matter.

CHAPTER THREE

THE TOUCH OF BREEZE

THE TOUCH OF BREEZE(PART-3)

Susmita could memorize like all happened a little earlier. They both liked hill stations so most of their tours were in hilly areas. Sometimes they went to the sea beach. They fought with each other and made arrangements very often because of Arijit's impatience mentality. Susmita tried a lot to adjust to Arijit but very often she also lost her patience. Little Ashish felt so scared because of Arijit's shouting. Sometimes they fought so hard that they skipped meals. Arijit took more sleeping pills (which were already in prescription) and slept the whole day without doing any work or taking food. Susmita had to go to school because it was a private school. She felt very happy to go there and she forgot everything while teaching the students. After fighting she went to school in tears and could not share it with her coworkers. For that reason, Arijit's business also got affected very much. His cousin's brother didn't like it long. At last their joint business stopped. When Arijit remained good he became a perfect gentleman. He knew lots of things. His memory was so sharp that he could easily remember all the old facts. After two or three days he became hot headed and then he lost all his good sense. Ashish had already got admission to a school. Then he was four years old. Only to meet up ends Susmita started private tuition at home. Her earnings increased more. Her mental strength also grew more.

Then Arijit started his own business and opened a cold drinks supply company in the name of his son. "The Ashish Enterprises".

Susmita helped him a lot to open it. She applied for a trade license and got it. She wanted from the heart to keep Arijit busy with his work.So that he could forget all his painful past. She kept the account up to date for the company. Sometimes in the evening, Arijit took her on his bike while collecting the money from the shops. He dreamed lots of things and said to Susmita very often " Ei , susmita you know, one day I will buy a big car and we will go on a long tour by car. The astrologer told my mom that I will do great in my drinks business". Arijit looked so beautiful while saying all. That time he gave Susmita two beautiful costly sarees together in every puja as a Puja gift. He bought a gift for his mom, Nipa and son Ashish.

When they argued they both became wild. Then Arijit became so violent that no one could stop him. Most of the time Arijit got furious with mom and to stop them Susmita also became a part of the fighting. He always used slang languages. One Sunday Nipa wanted to visit one of her sister-in-law Phulu's house with Susmita and Ashish. She invited all the relatives in her house for a function. She had arranged for a lunch party. Arijit hated her as she ruined his love with Mahua.

So he warrened Nipa by saying ,"Mom, you can go anywhere you wish. I don't have any problem with it. I have no power to stop you. In fact my dad also couldn't stop you. But don't take my wife and son in their house.Keep it in your mind and don't try to be over smart ". Then he went away on his bike for work. After seeing her mom in law sad and mourn Susmita decided to go there. That time Nipa didn't want to go anywhere without Ashish. Or maybe she loved Nipa more than Arijit. Later she did not get the reason! Why that day she disobeyed Arijit? That day was the first day when Arijit beat Susmita. After coming in the evening when Arijit understood it .He got very angry with his mom. And start shouting," You are the worst culprit in my life. You fucked up my life. My dad passed only for you. You cheated my dad by sleeping with Bhandaguru T. Chakraborty. And now you have taught Susmita to go against me! When I married her she was not like that. She understood my problems. For a few days I have been watching her trying to argue with me! "

His mom said," Your wife is an educated girl. She understands everything. She knows what is good or bad! I don't need to teach her. I didn't sleep with Guru. You are lying, all are your hallucinations. Ari doesn't say this".

He got more angry hearing all of it and slapped her hard, and said," I am lying ! Hun I am lying! You are a dirty woman. You forgot that day when I caught you and T .Chakraborty. Except Sunday that fake came every afternoon. And if I stayed at home not going to school by any chance you sent me to buy fruits for him.Can you remember it? My dad was an asshole . He never doubted you".

Then Susmita protested against it. She said,"Why are you talking like this in front of Ashish? Maybe Phulu Pisi spoiled your love life. But I don't have any business with it. She invited me so I showed my curtsy to meet her. There is no fault of mom. And mom's life is only her life. She did what she thought was good. Why are you trying lemon zest with it? "

He didn't like Susmita's opinion. He thought Susmita would support him. So he pushed and kicked Susmita to stop her. Then he went to his room and closed the door.Little Ashish started crying. It was the first time Arijit did this to her. She felt so ashamed to be insulted by him and thought of killing herself. She couldn't do it only for Ashish.Then in anger she started sleeping in Nipa's room. And fasted for two days .

After two days Arijit begged her mercy again and again. He grabbed her legs and said," Please Susmita forgive me. You know I become mad when I get angry.I take some chronic tablets. So I can't control myself.If you don't forgive me, or don't take your meal or don't sleep in our bed I will not leave your legs. I promise I will never do it".

Susmita had no option except to forgive him. But these types of things started happening every after ten or fifteen days.

Susmita was earning well and sometimes she thought about living in a rented house with her son. She knew Ashish loved her

Amma so much. From six months of age he slept in his granny's room with her. So it was not possible to get them apart from each other. Neither could she go to his parents in fear of society or in a different flat for Ashish and Nipa. At that time taking divorcerce and becoming a single parent was tough for a Bengali woman.

Susmita cried a lot and stopped her meal for three or four days if fought with Arijit. Then Nipa fed her forcefully and told her," Don't cry, my girl. It's your fortune. We can't deny it. Look at Ashish. You have to live only for him. Make him a good person. This is the only way to get peace in life. Don't expect anything from my son." When Arijit became normal he caught her feet again and said," Susmita please forgive me. This is the last time." And he also started crying" Poor Susmita forgot all by seeing him in this situation. She was grateful to him for getting Ashish. As then Ashish was the all source of happiness in her life. They behaved normally again as if nothing happened.

When Arijit behaved well Susmita felt very happy. They went out for dinner or sometimes he took Ashish and susmita on his bike and went to roam some famous places in Kolkata. But no one knew when he would get angry. So all the time Susmita felt scared. Though he was very romantic and very handsome. He was very fair and had a big broad hairy chest. When stayed at home he listened to beautiful songs by Rabindranath Tagore.

Susmita wanted to listen to a line from him to keep her head on his big chest. That was," Don't worry I am beside you" . But she never heard from him. Because Arijit did not have that strong mental position to say it. If he felt any problem he broke down badly.He was afraid to take any responsibility. His all power worked only on his mom and wife.Very often Susmita had to say " Don't worry ,I am beside you " to make him happy.

Three months before every holiday of Susmita's school he made a train reservation for travel. They didn't remain without fighting like normal couples.As if they thought of themselves as competitors of each other. That's why after a few years when Ashish became a teenager he didn't want to go with them.

Susmita never told her parents about her abnormal life. She didn't want to make them sad. All she hid in her soul. She started doing more tuition and kept herself busy with work. She thought lots of time not to have any argument with Arijit. But she couldn't agree with his wrong words. Especially about mom Nipa. So fighting was going on. When Arijit couldn't stop her he beat her. And that hurt her most.

She requested him lots of time, "Please don't beat me. My parents, my teachers never scolded me as I was so good. We can quarrel. And it happens in every family but don't do this. It is very painful for me". That day Arijit promised he would never do it.

In the time of Durga Puja Bengali people love to buy gifts for friends and relatives. They start their shopping two or three months before. Then Susmita had around fifty kids for private tuition.The guardians gave her various gifts. So she thought of buying some gifts for her students. One day one of the student's mom told her," Mam, you know if you buy from Barabazar(A marketplace of Kolkata, famous for various things) you will get it all at a very cheap rate. You know my husband goes there every week for his business. If you want to go then I and you can go with him. I also have to buy something."

Susmita said," Thank you so much for the information. Let me ask my mom-in-law. Then we will decide the day".

That market remains closed on Sunday. She thought to go there on one Saturday and

Susmita asked Nipa," Mom you know Kunal's mom told me in Barabazar everything is very cheap. I have to buy lots of gifts. So what do you think? Should I go there?"

Nipa said "Yes, I know about that market. Your dad's office was near that market. I went there with him. It is true all are cheap but they don't sell one piece and you have to buy a dozen. Yes, you can go, don't worry I will take care of Ashish."

Susmita said ," Mom not only Ashish , you have to look after Kunal also. Because Kunal's mom, me, and her dad will go ".

Nipa replied," Aree baba, it's okay don't think so much. It will be my pleasure to keep both of them. You go but ask Ari also. If he wants to go with you or not"?

At night Susmita told Arijit," Ei Listen, tomorrow I am going to Barabazar with Kunal's parents to buy some gifts. Will you go with us?"

Arijit said, " You know I don't have that much tolerance. If I spend hour to hour I know I will suffer from a headache. (That time Arijit was suffering from a headache problem). You go with whom you want but don't request me either".

So the next morning Kunal's dad came around 10 AM with Kunal on his bike to keep her in charge of Nipa and said to Susmita," Didi (Elder sister) if you are ready you can sit on my bike then you don't need to walk to the bus stand. Kunal's mom is waiting there. After keeping my bike in the parking center we will catch the bus." Susmita thought it would be great that she didn't need to walk to the bus stand. So saying 'bye bye' to Nipa and Arijit she sat on Kunal dad's bike.

She bought lots of gifts. They ate lunch in a restaurant .In the evening she and Kunal's mom came home together by walking from the bus stop. Kunal's dad had something to do so he dropped them off at the bus stop and went to work.

From that day Arijit stopped talking to her. She couldn't understand anything. She thought maybe his mood was not good. He had a mood swing problem. Monday morning before going to school she caught his hand and said," Hey ,I am going to school. Last two days you haven't talked to me. You didn't want to see the gifts. What happened to you? Are you okay"?

CHAPTER FOUR

THE TOUCH OF BREEZE

THE TOUCH OF BREEZE(PART-4)

Suddenly Arijit roared at her," Don't touch me! You are a loose character woman! You are from a low family that's why your nature is like that. Where have you gone to fuck sitting on his bike? Did You hold him back "?

Susmita was surprised by hearing his dirty words. She thought he was having fun to irritate Susmita.She laughed and said," Are you jealous of him! You always say no one will like me as I am dark. And now you are saying all! Listen, he respects me as his son's teacher. He calls me Didi. Why should I touch him ? What are you saying? No I didn't touch him, I caught the seat edge. Now I don't have time to tell you all. I will be late to school." Saying that she went to school.

Susmita couldn't take classes in the school with a peaceful mind. She was very worried. She saw how Arijit was furious with her.

When she came back home at noon she heard Arijit saying to his mom," Mom, tell her to leave our house.There is no place for a characterless woman here. I promised not to hit her. Otherwise yesterday I would end the story. I am not like my dad, like a coward".

Nipa never had dared to talk against him. She never punished him or scolded him for his mistakes. She only supported him blindly or tried to stop him. Maybe she felt guilty about her son. She only said," If I tell her to leave this house what will the neighbors say? Ashish loves me but if he doesn't see her mom for long he will cry".

Arijit was adamant. He threatened his mom," If you don't tell her to leave then I will destroy all the idols of your God and Goddess. Do you want to see? "

Every early morning Nipa worshiped her Gods and Goddess for around one hour. It gave her a kind of pleasure. If by any chance she couldn't do it, she didn't get peace.

Susmita felt so helpless about her mom-in-law. She felt more sorry for Nipa. Arijit insulted her in so many ways. But she never thought about any man in her life except Arijit. She felt pity on him. She thought if she stayed out of his sight for a few days Arijit would become calm again.

So she decided to leave home and go to her parent's house. Before that Arijit did not like to let her live with her parents for one night.If she went there she had to come back at night.

Her school was near her house. She went to school on foot. Ashish was in class one.She didn't take Ashish with her to her parent's house. Because when she would come to school her mom would not take care of him. Only his Amma Nipa could make him good. Above all Ashish's couldn't be able to go to school. So before leaving she hugged Ashish and said, " Babu , I am going to Didan's house(Ashish called Susmita's mom, Didan).I have something to do. I will not return tonight. Don't be naughty with your Amma ".

Ashish said," Mom, I want to go with you". Arijit shouted and said," No you don't need to go". Ashish was afraid of his dad. He became silent. Susmita left home with tears and said in her mind ," Arijit, you tried to abuse me in many ways.You fraud me not telling me the truth before marriage and I adjusted with all only for your illness. Today what you have done I never will forget it and I never will forgive you for this reason in my whole life".

Susmita came to her parent's house. Seeing her without any prior notice her parents were surprised. Her mom asked," Why didn't you bring Bhaiya? (Susmita's mom called Ashish in the name of Bhaiya means brother) What happened to you? Are you good?"

" Yes Mom, I am good. Ashish didn't want to come here without his Amma. I thought about staying here for a few days. Do you have any problems?" Susmita said. Her mom understood something wrong had happened.

In the very early morning, Susmita got up and got ready for school. Then she took the bus and came to school. Then she came to Arijit's house to visit Ashish and spent some time with him. After that she did her private tuition in a student's home. In the evening she returned to her parents. Ashish didn't want to leave her. He cried and Susmita also cried. After one week Ashish felt sick. Ashish was very weak from his birth. He had a fever very often. So Susmita came back from her parent's house. Arijit didn't oppose anything.

Susmita came back but they both stopped talking to each other. They didn't sleep on the same bed. Susmita, Ashish

and Nipa slept in Nipa's room. Arijit got more violent. Every day he tried to fight with Susmita or Nipa without any reason. He had a doubt in mind that Susmita had some affairs with Kunal's dad. But God knew then only Arijit was in her life.

Only to remove his doubt Nipa told her, "Susmita, please don't make him angry anymore. I talked to him. If you stop giving tuition to Kunal then this doubt will go from his mind". "What are you saying, Mom? I didn't do anything wrong. And how can I tell them that I will not teach Kunal? He loves me and Ashish very much. And why should I appreciate his dirty thoughts? I can't do it. I am a teacher, I teach children to follow the right way now I have to support the narrow things." Susmita replied.

" Listen to me, Susmita. Sometimes we need to do something for peace in life. The experience made my hair white. I will handle it all. You know Ari is suffering from Ocd. And making doubt is one of the parts of it. I will make Kunal's parents understand. You don't need to worry." Nipa said, "So one day when Arijit was not at home Nipa called them and said," Please don't mind. Susmita will not teach your son anymore. One of my neighbors made a bad comment about seeing her on your bike and my son got very angry."

They were shocked and speechless.

Kunal's mom said," What a shame! I just can't think people can be so mean-minded. We are sorry for madam. Kunal loves her teacher very much.We don't know what we will say to him ? That is very sad."

After they were gone, Susmita felt so ashamed. Her tears came thinking that why did all the mess Arijit made intentionally or for his illness? The problem was solved temporarily.

After around one month Arijit first talked to her,"Susmita I know I did wrong but trust me I tried not to doubt you. My heart knows you can't do any wrong but my brain didn't listen to my heart. My Ocd forced me to think over and over that you touched him. I did not remove this thought from my mind. Thousands of my trying.Please forget all and forgive me last time. Let's start from a new beginning. Let's go to Simla during Puja vacation. So get ready". He begged her mercy again and again.

Susmita was not so hard. She always wanted to get his love and a beautiful family like others. So she became weak again. Though Arijit was mentally ill he was physically very strong. So the sexual relationship between them was very good. They went to Simla during the Puja vacation.

Before that Nipa went to a famous lady psychiatrist of the city without telling Arijit and told her the problems of Arijit. She gave him some medicines which Nipa and Susmita gave him mixed with food hiding from him. After taking those medicines his attitude changed. When he became normal he was like a child and he had lots of outside knowledge that Susmita loved truly.

One year passed so quickly. They went to Bhutan during the next Summer vacation. Susmita's earnings increased a lot. That time most of the expenditure on the tour was given by Susmita. Arijit only cut the tickets. Arijit didn't like package tours. He loved to go with his own responsibility. This was the only thing that he could do perfect. Nipa didn't like their tour very much.Arijit didn't want to listen to anything against it. He loved to see the new city and so did Susmita also.

Before going to Bhutan Susmita opposed and said, "Listen, last year we went to Simla. Now we have to think about our future.About Ashish . If we spend so much money in this way, what will happen next?"

Arijit laughed and told her," Life is for once so live it fully. See the world. Make your memories full with beautiful experiences of tours. So that one day you can remember how beautiful the world is! You don't need to think about anyone. All live on their luck. It is Ashish's life. We don't know what is waiting for him. We can only make him an educated person, nothing else. And I can't deny that you are doing your best to make him a good person. I know I don't do anything. You know Susmita, what hurts me? When I see my younger brothers or friends have done something great, and I am a failure person even though I had that ability then I feel an inferiority complex. Then I can't control myself. All my anger goes to my mom. That she couldn't raise me well. You know, before starting the Sanchayi company ,we had a small and beautiful family. My dad was a central government employee. Financially we were strong. Every year my dad's office provided a free trip for the family. And from childhood, my dad took us to so many places. Life was so beautiful then. My mom is beautiful as is my dad. You know how beautiful my sister is! We both were good at studying. All our relatives were jealous of us. When my dad met with T chakraborty from that time our bad luck started. That's why I am saying life is full of miracles."

"You can't change them. We need to live in the present. Don't you understand that?" Susmita said.

" I know Susmita, I know everything. We can't ignore our past. All are related to the present. You know my mom read only up to class six. So she didn't oppose my dad's decision to leave his government job. She only cooked a good meal for us and took great care of household work. But never paid any attention to our study. That's why I thought I don't need a beautiful wife, I need an educated woman as my life partner. So I have chosen you. You know my youngest aunt Mita Masi(Bengali people call maternal aunt Masi) every evening came to our house with her boyfriend and spent time with him in front of us when we were reading. And it affected our study very much. But my mom never told her anything. You know I wanted to be a doctor. My dad didn't want it.If my mom made him understand to let me fulfill my dream then the history of my life would be different. Unfortunately, you are educated but you don't understand me. I can't blame you only because I made a mistake by doing an arranged marriage instead of a love marriage. You didn't know anything about me before marriage so you never will realize my pain. Actually you have no fault. You want me as a normal person like others but I lost those days at the age of 22. Now I think a love marriage is better than an arranged marriage. When I caught my mom's affair with Bhandaguru I was shocked. I didn't believe my eyes.I thought about my mom, whom I love so much, how she could do this type of thing?My dad loved my mom very much. They never argued like us. How could my mom have cheated on him? From that day I started believing Maybe women are like that. These things didn't have any effect on my sister's life. She got married and went with her husband to Delhi. Only I became a patient of Ocd and an ugly man in front of society who always shouts at home. I know I don't behave like a normal man. I know that, you blame your luck and regret. You think why this happens to you? What can I do? My luck will join with someone, maybe not with you. I am a different type." He looked so sad saying everything.

CHAPTER FIVE

THE TOUCH OF BREEZE

THE TOUCH OF BREEZE(PART-5)

Susmita felt sorry she didn't understand what to say. She knew all these things. Arijit felt relieved by saying all. He said," You know Susmita,when I travel anywhere I forget my surroundings .Then I dreamt of living a new way." Susmita did not deny and she agreed to go to Bhutan and went there.

Arijit appointed a helper and a staff for collecting money. He took a rented godown except of their house. His business was going good. He stopped going to shops to collect money. If he went on sun he had a headache problem and he took lots of pain killers. Susmita took him to Bangalore for his headache problem. After the test nothing came bad.Though Arijit thought he had a migraine.It was actually a part of his depression.

Ashish got admission to class 5.One day when Susmita was mixing the medicine at Arijit's dinner in a bowl of dal(pulses). By chance, he saw it. He became fierce and howled,

" What the hell are you combining with my food? Mom, Mom! come and see what she is doing? Tell me the truth now. Otherwise I will destroy everything. You know I don't like cleverness. ". Saying that he threw the bowl on the wall.

Nipa kept her hands on his head and said," Ari, Ari, my boy please calm down. All are for your good my boy. We are not your enemy. We want to cure you".

" Really ! Is it ! If you want that my life will not be miserable. I want to know the truth. Now say? Who will tell me ? You or she?"

Arijit cried out.

Susmita said in fear," This is a medicine to cure your distrustful illness. Mom went to a psychiatrist with Pisimoni (Arijit's youngest aunt). She gave it to you". And she showed the bottle to him.

"What! I am taking lots of pills already. I read the group. Oh! My God! That's why I don't feel energetic. I feel physically weak all the time. Mom, how could you do it with me? How dare you? I never trusted you. I don't trust Susmita either. What do you think? Medicine can change my views? No, no! you made Susmita a liar also like you. Today I will show you how far I can go. I will destroy everything .You started the story and I will end it." He started breaking things. He hit his mom so hard that she fell on the ground. Ashish started crying in fear. Susmita came to save Nipa. Then Arijit attacked her and started beating her. She couldn't control her. This is the first time she slapped him. Then he became more violent. He never thought Susmita could slap him ever.

He said rudely. " You slapped me! How dare you? My mom never did that! Get out right now from this house otherwise I will kill myself".

Nipa knew her son's anger so she took Ashish's hand and said to Susmita," Let's go to your parent's house. I can't let you go alone tonight with Ashish. Let him live alone. Come hurry up. Now it is ten p.m. If we get late we will not get any vehicle to go.

Before leaving, Nipa went to her brother Barun's house which was next door. Seeing her in this condition her brother said," Didi, you don't go anywhere. This house is made by your husband. I never wanted to interfere in your family life. I hear all but I keep silent.You are responsible for all . Only for your indulgence Ari became so adamant. But today I can't tolerate it anymore. Ari needs a lesson".

He called some other neighbors and entered their house. One of the old people slapped Arijit and said," Don't you feel shameful for your behavior? You aren't illiterate. How could you beat the women? You have a so cute son. Your wife is a teacher. We feel proud of her. She came from outside but in her own effort she got a job.You have a beautiful small family. You are not satisfied with everything. We all know only for you they all are unhappy."

Susmita was feeling bad as the outsiders interface in their life. But that day without it no one could stop Ariji. She told them, "Please, you people go. Let us solve our own problems."

Arijit was silent. He couldn't imagine that the neighbors could come.

His uncle said," This is not your house. You didn't do anything for it. I know how my brother in law made this house. When Sanchayee collapsed. You did not want to come to this village from Kolkata. Then you didn't even come to see it. You get out of this house. Listen,don't try to make any mess anymore." Then he left.

His dad bought the land in that village. He made this house only to get rid of house rent in Kolkata. Before his dad's death Arijit didn't want to come to that village. So they lived in Kolkata in a rented house. After his dad's death they came here. After Nipa's death Susmita sold that house and came to Jadavpur.

After the neighbor went that night, except Ashish no one had a meal. Arijit took lots of sleeping pills and fell asleep. The next morning Susmita had to go school. Because the examinations were going on. She had to guard the exam hall. All were sleeping, Susmita went to school. The school was one of the happiest places in her life. All the colleagues loved her. She was very popular as a good teacher. She never told anyone about her painful life.The school management committee liked her most as a serious and responsible teacher. She was not deceitful. Everywhere, maybe in school or household work, no one could defeat her. She was very hard-working and loved to laugh loudly and had a very positive mentality. But she had to cry most of the time. Nipa told her lots of times to leave Arijit. But why didn't she do that, it was a mystery. Actually she was timid. She felt afraid to take risks. She was an overthinker who was not courageous enough to take decisions about her life.

After coming home she found that Arijit left the house. From his worker they knew that he had taken a rented house a little far. Their house became a peaceful place after he was gone. Nipa and Susmita both knew he would not bear oily and spicy food from outside long as he took lots of medicines. One day Nipa called his helper, Sanu, to know about Arijit. Sanu told them," Ari Da is good but he is tense". He said secretly to Susmita," Boudi(the wife of brother), Ari da is not well. I lied to aunty. He takes lots of painkillers and sleeps the whole day. He doesn't take food properly. Boudi, I request you to bring him back home, otherwise he will get sick soon. You know, Ari da is very adamant he will prefer death instead of coming back by himself".

Susmita became very anxious. She was afraid of his temper.

One month gone Susmita felt sorry for Arijit. She knew he used to take lots of costly medicines. Which Susmita bought for him. She knew Arijit had not earned enough to manage all. He had to pay salary for his two staff, Godown rent, house rent, food, and medicines. So she thought of meeting him. She loved him but was afraid of him also.

One day she met him in the rented house. Seeing her Arijit became so happy. He hugged her and started kissing her madly and said to Susmita," I will die without you and Ashish . I don't want to go back to my home where these types of neighbors and relatives live. Every day I cry for you and my son. He is my life. Susmita, please let me live. That day I lost my senses. My mom screwed my life. I got you and thought of a new life. It is also going to finish. Susmita, please help me. You know how painful my life is". Again she couldn't deny his love. She also kissed him. They both were hungry for physical relations. Arijit was very manly. His love was wild which Susmita missed a lot. They had sex there. Then she promised to Arijit that she would come to him with Ashish.

After coming home she said to Nipa," Mom, today I visited Arijit. He is not well. He doesn't want to come back here. He wants me to stay with him in the rented house. I don't know what to do"?

Nipa said," Susmita save my son, please. Only you can do it. Go and stay with him.Don't take Ashish for long. Then I will die. And slowly try to make Ari agree to come here."

Susmita and Arijit started living together in the rented house. She took Arijit to a new Physiatrist. And he was doing well. Their rented house was half an hour away from Nipa's house. After school, she went to Nipa. She and Ashish spent a few times with her. Only on holidays, she left Ashish to Nipa for whole days.Days were passing by. The first few days Arijit bought groceries or vegetables but then he went back to his old form. That time was very good for them. They lived freely without interference from Nipa.

After around eight months one day suddenly Nipa became unconscious. Doctor told her she had some heart problems. She needed full rest. So they came back again.

There was a marriage ceremony for Barun's daughter. Only to avoid this occasion Arijit cut tickets to Haridwar. He went to Badrinath also. He requested Susmita, a lot to go with him. But Susmita did not go with him, because she thought of other relatives. What would they think? She also knew that night Barun's uncle didn't make any mistake. Rather he helped from disaster. So Arijit went alone.

Before going he said to Susmita," You also are worried about society or people like my mom. You never gave importance after your love. You forgot the bows we had taken while getting married. I thought you would like to have company with me." Susmita was silent that time. Nipa didn't want Susmita to support Arijit's plan.

She enjoyed the marriage ceremony with other relatives. Her mind didn't get peace thinking about Arijit. He came back and became ill. There he didn't take care of himself properly. Susmita felt so regretful for it.

One day it was a birthday invitation of one of her students. Susmita went there with Ashish. Arijit didn't want to go anywhere. Her name was Debosmita. Her mom Tania took great care of them. Susmita was surprised to see her disabled son. She thought Debosmita was Tania's only daughter. Susmita said to her," Tania , sorry I didn't know you have a son. Otherwise I will bring a gift for him". Tania started crying and said," Didi, God made him like that. I also did wrong. No gift can change my poor boy's life.You know his dad Madav was my first husband. It was an arranged marriage. After three years of marriage I gave birth to him. His dad had a transferable job.After marriage I went with him to Punjab. Those days were like the dream days of my life. Every weekend we roamed to famous places in Dehradun by his car. In those three years we went ten times on our honeymoon in different places of India. After one year of my son's birth we realized that he had some problems. I came to Kolkata to my in-law's house for his treatment. His dad also came.He had to go back for his work.That time one of his close friends helped me a lot in my son's treatment.His name was Tanmoy. I was tired from doing all the duties alone. His treatment was going on. There was no development. On the other hand my husband got transferred to Rajasthan. He did not have enough time for his son. Four years gone in this way. In the meantime, Tanmoy and I fell in love. My heart wanted freedom. I couldn't take it anymore. So one day I fled with Tanmoy and got married. I left my son to my in-laws. When my husband knew it all he came to meet us. He scolded Tanmoy as a traitor. He pleaded with me again and again to come back to him. I had nothing to do.He never married again. He doesn't come to Kolkata. He sends money every month. My ex dad in law has died so mom in law looks after my son. Occasionally I bring him here to Tanmoy's house. Now I feel sorry that my son is living like an orphan. Didi ,what could I do? That time I found peace in Tanmoy. My peace had gone forever. Tommy's parents also cursed me for fucking up their only son's life. Every time I feel guilty for my work. Tanmoy also fed up on me. I can't sleep without pills".

CHAPTER SIX

THE TOUCH OF BREEZE

THE TOUCH OF BREEZE(PART-6)

Susmita hugged her and said," Don't think in this way please. Don't hurt yourself. Whatever happens, just accept it. Live your life without regret. Take care of your son and daughter equally as much as you can. You are brave. I believe that every woman has the power to handle all".

While coming from their home Susmita was thinking, what Tina had done! Susmita never thought to do it. Arijit insulted her lots of times. She never thought to cheat him.

Life was going as usual for Susmita. Arijit's business was not going well. He only depended on workers. For that reason he always remained tense. Nothing felt good to him. He didn't like to hear about anyone's good news. Susmita's cousin sister was Atasi. She loved a guy. His name was Arjun.

One day Arjun met with Atasi's parents and told them that he loves Atasi and he would marry her after getting a government job.

He tried hard for a few years to get a government job. At last he got a central government job in rail. When Arijit knew about it he didn't believe it. He said Arjun was lying. He thought that he couldn't do anything good so no one could do it. Susmita argued with him about it.

One day Arjun brought his parents to meet with Atasi's parents And both the families fixed a date of their marriage.

Susmita was very happy about Atasi. Though she was her cousin's sister, she thought her own sister and loved her very much.

She took lots of responsibility for the wedding.

Atasi got married to Arjun. Susmita sometimes felt very jealous to see their beautiful love bonding. Arjun was a family man. Arijit was never like that. It hurt Susmita a lot. Only her happiness was in her job as a teacher and her son Ashish. Arijit didn't want to go to any relative's house or any invitation. Instead of going anywhere, he loved to sleep in peace. Susmita had to maintain all the formalities. She went everywhere with Ashish. Nipa was not able to go because of her knee pain and heart problems. Susmita wanted from the heart Arijit's company.She couldn't request him more as he was very ill-tempered. Sometimes If she requested more then he said,

"I don't like nagging. I am like myself and you have to accept it. And I think you already got it. If I don't have some disabilities I would not marry a dark girl like you".

Susmita had nothing to say. At a family function someone asked her ,'Why didn't Arijit come"? She lied and said, " He is busy with work and so on". She never wanted to put him down in front of all. She felt bad for Arijit . She did not dare to make a boyfriend or not have any interest in it. Though lots of her friends had extra meritorious relationships.

When Arijit got angry he insulted her or tried to show her down in many ways. Then she had only her tears and Ashish gave her comfort. Every early morning she prayed to God to make everything normal in her life. But that time God was as if dumb and deaf.

When they both quarreled Ashish also tried to keep her silent like Nipa. Arijit couldn't remain at peace without fighting for long. For his chronic illness. Though he promised lots of time not to make any mess but couldn't keep it. He hated his dad very much. And he tried to prove himself better than him.

Susmita realized how a small wrong decision makes people's life like hell. Bengali women call their husbands' Bor‘.' Bor 'means blessings. But Arijit never became a 'Bor‘ in Susmita's life. He stayed as Ashish's dad.

Ashish was promoted to class eight . He became a handsome and smart man. All said he looked like his dad.He was very fair like Arijit. But he was just the opposite to his dad. He talked very little. And he was a cool headed boy. Arijit had pride in him. Nipa became weaker. Arijit's business was not going well. He didn't have any interest in continuing it. His assistant and staff did this. He took a rest at home.

On the other hand Susmita became very famous as an English teacher. In the meantime, Arijit's feet were swollen . One day he became unconscious. Then Susmita was in school. Nipa gave her the news through a neighbor. She came hurriedly. They admitted him to the hospital. He was diagnosed with heart problems and diabetes. His heartbeat became slow. The doctor prescribed him some medicines. And strictly told him not to drink more than one to two liters of water in a whole day. Arijit drank lots of water. After coming back home from hospital he was not able to run his business anymore. He made a huge loss. Nipa was forced to sell one of their lands at a very low price to repay the debt. The business got closed. Arijit became more impatient by sitting all the time at home. All the financial burden came over Susmita.

Susmita started her day very early in the morning and after doing household chores she took a bath and did her daily worship of God. Then she wore her saree and got ready for school. She never did any makeup because she didn't feel happy inside and didn't get enough time before going to school .

Her colleagues always said to her," Susmita may be dark but she looks so beautiful in her simplicity. With makeup she will look more beautiful ". Her face was very cute. She was very slim and had long hair. In her school all were lady teachers except the drawing teacher. When the ladies talked about their husbands in the teacher's room or their work pressure of their love and their caring attitude. She felt very ashamed to say that her husband was a workless person. Sometimes she wondered why she got married. Those days her little cousin's sister Sudesna also got married. It was also a love marriage.

When they went traveling her friends felt jealous. One of her best friends was Oindrila . She often said to her," Susmita you are very lucky to have such a romantic husband who takes you on your honeymoon two times a year". Susmita kept her silent except for smiling

There was only one person with whom she shared all the truth, and that was God. Sometimes she asked Him," What did I do with you? Why do you punish me so hard? From my childhood I didn't get anything as I wished. Didn't I deserve a normal man as a husband? My two cousin's sisters got married and you gave them a happy life. I am happy for them. Am I your enemy? I am tired of acting. I can't fight anymore. When will I get freedom from it?"

After coming home from school she quickly took her lunch and took a nap then she sat for private tuition. She finished it in the evening. At night she cooked dinner. So sometimes she became very intolerant.

The whole day Arijit wanted tea ten or twelve times. He behaved like a child. What he said once all had to obey it. He didn't have a proper lunch like rice or roti at noon. He wanted some special dishes. It was hectic for Susmita and Nipa. Every day they had to think about what special they could make for him. He only ordered and if they couldn't arrange he skipped his meal. Nipa got very angry with Susmita if he didn't take his food. He didn't listen to the doctor. He always ran his life in his way. He drank water without limitations. He took sleeping pills without a prescription whenever he wanted. All things made Susmita very worried about his health. His temper was always high.

He often said," I don't want to make my life long. I know I am a failure. If I live or die that will not affect anyone". Susmita felt sad but she had nothing to do. She was also working hard to run the family well. The only thing that made him happy was going on trips. So later she arranged for it to make him happy with her own money. Then her responsibility works more than her love.

Ashish passed his class twelve and got admission in engineering. Nipa's little sister Mita's only daughter Moumita became a doctor.

Arijit didn't like the news. He didn't like Mita as she once disturbed their study life. Moumita's marriage was fixed with a doctor guy. So one day Mita and her husband came to invite them. They praised that doctor guy a lot. After they were gone Arijit felt very vicious from heart and roared," I will never go there. Aunt is so shameless. Though she is my aunt but never felt sorrow about my life. When we were small she spoiled our studies. In front of us, she used to play with her lover. Her daughter's study or exam time didn't allow anyone to go to her house. Mom, have you seen your sister? How much pride she showed you. Don't you feel ashamed that your only son is living on his wife's mercy? Mom, what can I say to you now at this age? My whole life fucked up. I hate my life. And now medicines are my lifeline".

Susmita caught his hand and hugged him. She tried to stop him saying," Please Don't say this. This is not the end of the world. Maybe it was Your luck. But God has gifted you a family and a son." That day also he took his pills and went to sleep without taking his meal. That time he was taking an overdose of anti-anxiety pills without obeying the doctor. He was very adamant from childhood. Susmita very often said to him,"Don't take too many pills without a prescription. It will harm your health".

He replied," Listen, I know more than my doctor about mental illness. Because I am suffering from it every day."

On Moumita's marriage day, he didn't go but he wasn't opposed to going to Susmita and Nipa.At night when they got back home. He cried out to Susmita," Why did you go there? Don't you feel bad for me? What type of wife are you? Then what is the meaning of love? My dad was an idiot. He let my mom do everything.I am not like him. I always say you are from the lower class! And see you have proved it. If I will be in your place I will never go there. My mom is also like that."

Susmita just said," But you didn't say anything before going! And now!" He slapped her on the face and said," How dare you argue with me! I hate you. You went there without me. I made the mistake of marrying you! I thought you were soft-hearted but you are cruel.

You always treat me as a normal man knowing well that I am going through a tough time. I don't want to live anymore." Going to the bedroom that night he took twenty sleeping pills together and tried to kill himself. He tried to commit suicide before.

They admitted him to an asylum center. When he got conscious he didn't want to stay there a minute.He requested the doctor to leave him. When Susmita met him he caught her hands and said," Please forgive me. I did wrong. I can't stay here alone without you all. Sometimes my brain doesn't work .I messed up. Please take me home." Susmita said," I will certainly take you home but here are some rules. We have to follow it. Before forty days they will not leave you. You don't follow the prescription. Here they will treat you and set your routine normal. Please cooperate with the doctors." She came back in tears.

After forty days he came back from asylum. He became quite calm and physically weak.Their physical relationship was not usual as a couple it never became normal. After that, he took a job at a private company as Susmita always forced him but didn't continue long for his health.

Then suddenly he passed away making her free from all burdens. Susmita couldn't do anything to save him. A sudden cerebral attack and all finished. He didn't give her a chance to fight against it. On the way to the hospital he died. In the ambulance, he caught Susmita's hand tightly. When he was gone, Susmita made her hands untied from him with tears in her eyes. He always made Susmita suffer for him but in the end, he just left her very casually.That time Ashish was in fourth year.

CHAPTER SEVEN

THE TOUCH OF BREEZE

THE TOUCH OF BREEZE(PART-7)

Nipa was also alive then. Last few years of her life she cried for her son. Though for Ashish she always felt proud.

She was bedridden then. Susmita did a lot for her. Before death, one day she blessed Susmita and said ," You are the Lakshmi (The Goddess of wealth)of my family. But you were Saraswati (The Goddess of creativity) too. I bless you from my heart, one day you will be a great one. Forgive me and my son for being unfair to you".

Susmita said," Mom please stop. Don't say it like this. You forgive me. I also did wrong".

Nipa couldn't hear anything. She continued," I always tried to control my son's life . I felt jealous when you went on tour. I know most of the time you fought with him only for me. When you both quarreled I always took his side knowing he was doing wrong. Believe me I only did it to make him happy. My son was brilliant but failed to do anything only for us so I never wanted to get him angry. He told you lots of time to leave this house but you never left us. He knew you would never leave us forever as you love us.You did a lot for us but my son didn't value you. As a woman, I can understand how painful it is for a woman by getting a husband like him. If you get someone normal you will be a great wife.He was sick.I know he loved you very much. He didn't know how to show his gratitude to you. Because he thought men should be manly. He told me lots of times behind you, "Mom, I am fortunate to have her in my life. I respect her patience. I haven't given her anything except sorrow.If she wanted to divorce me she could easily but she didn't. She always tried to keep us happy by taking all the responsibility".

Susmita kept her palm on her mouth and said, "Mom, please stop. He has gone. And I have forgiven him. I don't know if he would ever forgive me or not for my sins. I didn't get a chance to beg for his forgiveness ".

After Ashish's marriage, Nipa died. Then Susmita came to Jadavpur selling their old house. That place was more comfortable for her writing. Memorizing Nipa and those days her tears were rolling down through her cheeks .Arijit always wanted more concentration and sympathy from her. Susmita couldn't do it properly. Last few years they slept on the same bed but Susmita didn't let Arijit touch her. A hatred grew in her mind for him. Sometimes he wanted a physical relationship. But she was not interested.

One day Arijit told her," Susmita, why don't you let me touch you? You know your touch makes me sleep well. After marriage, you loved my big hairy chest. When you kept your hand on my heart and rotated it on my chest, those feelings I can't express by words".

All those words are now a memory in her life. Maybe she didn't love Arijit unconditionally or maybe she cheated on him. Arijit loved her. That time she was madly in love with Samir. She didn't know if Arijit realized it or not but a kind of guilt still worked in her mind. After Ariijit was gone she touched his feet and prayed to him," Arijit, I am a cheater.I didn't keep the oath that I took while married to you.That we will always remain loyal to each other. Forgive me for my betrayal otherwise, I will not forgive myself "

The train was running at high speed. Susmita saw on her phone it was almost morning at 5AM .All were sleeping.She tried to close her eyes and slowly she fell asleep.

When she opened her eyes it was almost twelve-thirty o'clock at noon. Ashish told her," Mom good morning. What happened to you? Are you okay? You never slept so long. Silpa tried to wake you up but I stopped her. Mom, do you want tea"? Silpa laughed and said," I know Granny was dreaming of Dadan.Is this true Granny ?". Rina told Silpa," Hush! Always too much talk".

Susmita felt a little embarrassed and said," Aree no, I am good. I fell asleep around 5 a.m. Actually the bed has changed so my sleep has gone. No, no I don't want tea now. I will have lunch. It's already late."

Susmita went to the washroom. Coming back to their seat she found lunch being served. She had a veg meal with rice, dal, a mix of vegetable curry, two chapatis, papad, and curd. After finishing lunch Silpa and she sat together.

Rina told her mom in law "Mom, I and Ashish like to take a nap. Silpa got up late. Now you both spend time," They slept in their berth.

Silpa asked," Granny, how do you write such beautiful stories? Where do you get the plot?"

Susmita said with a smile" Do you like my stories? I take the plot around us. All are based on true stories I only write with my little imagination."

" Granny ,do you know my friends always say that you are an excellent woman? Dad was also saying that you are a real fighter in life. I read your many stories. Some of them are very touchy."Silpa replied.

Susmita said," Leave my story. I want to hear Didibhai's real story (Susmita calls her Didibhai). Tell me who is that guy with whom you talk secretly".

Silpa answered, " Uff Granny,I know you will not leave me. He is Rik. Two years older than me. Studying medicine. He is a very good student. Very handsome to look at. And a very caring and adjustable mentality. So I liked him. You know I can't compromise with anything. Dad says I am like my Dadan.Is it right Granny?"

" Yes darling, you look like him. Very fair. He had big eyes. I always said it was like a cow's eyes. Your eyes are also like that". Susmita replied.

Silpa asked ," Granny, how did you meet Dadan? Love marriage?"

Susmita replied," No sweetheart, purely arranged marriage. We didn't know each other before marriage".

" Granny , Mom also had arranged marriage? I don't understand how two people get married without knowing each other. O, my God! I just can't think it can happen till now. How can they adjust with each other?" Silpa asked.

Susmita replied," It happened a few years ago. But now the time has changed. Now arranged marriage is rare. But I think whether it is love or arranged marriage. Adjustment is necessary everywhere. Now you are sixteen. You will understand it after a few years".

Silpa asked," Granny , do you know how mom and dad get to know each other? I never saw them fight. They have such similarities. They are the best couple in front of me."

Susmita said," Indeed, they are a beautiful couple. Your dad was two years older than your mom. As I know they had a common group of seven friends. They studied in the same school. And then they became close. Your dad first brought your mom to our house after two weeks of your Dadan's gone. Then your dad was doing his engineering. After the first meeting, I understood Rina was a very good girl ".

Silpa said," Wow! That's great. You didn't say anything to dad?"

Susmita replied," No ,my darling. I never interfere in your dad's life. I believe in freedom. I only told him to decide carefully so that he didn't have to regret it. Mithi, this advice is for you also".

Silpa said," Yes, Granny , you are right. A small wrong decision can make our life miserable. You know my best friend Debolina read your book 'Touch of Sky '. She was overwhelmed. She wanted to know how you started your writing "? Now I will do a video recording. And I will take your interview. Don't say' no' please. It is my prestige issue." Susmita laughed and said,' Accha baba, ok. ok. This credit goes to your dad. After your Dadan's gone I felt very lonely. Despite my school and tuition, I had to do lots of things for him. But suddenly everything stopped. I cried very often. So your dad told me,' Mom you like to write. There is an international platform where you can express your feelings by writing! My writing journey began. Slowly I modified myself. From short stories, I started writing novels, poems. Then my book was published. That's it. Silpa recorded everything. Then Silpa said ,'' You know some of your stories are so real as if it was your personal experience! What about them?"

Susmita said, " A writer can write on various things with or without experience. I think at first a writer writes from personal feelings but after a few years, it isn't needed. But yes of course when it comes from personal experience that is certainly good. Didibhai, take some rest. We have been talking for a long time."

Silpa said,'' Granny! You know. I miss you a lot In Mumbai. Why don't you stay with us forever? After every exam, I wanted to come to you in Kolkata but mom didn't want to leave me alone. Last two years Mom only said to concentrate on my board exam. So we didn't come to you. Only dad alone visited you. After my board, dad told me,' Let's go to Granny in this Durga Puja. We will stay there for one week and then with Granny we will go straight to Haridwar and from there we will visit Harsil and Gangotree and if you can travel then if we get a chance we can trek to Gomukh , Tapovan also.You know I was so surprised. I hugged Dad immediately. I was so happy".

Susmita said ," Oh! That is! Your dad is like that. He loves to surprise others. He called me over the phone and said 'Mom, we are coming there. And get ready for Hariddwar. Silpa is excited to take you with us. So don't say no. Her heart will break.He surprised me. The first time he brought your mom to our house then she was just a young girl. Before that he always said there is no special one in his life. Ashish's Amma was alive. She loved your dad very much. Only she had a little objection about your mom's height. Asha's Amma was very tall. And she liked tall people. You know after that I realized I had to renovate our old house. So we bought a new home in Jadavpur. Ashish's Amma wanted to meet Rina's parents and fixed the marriage between them".

Silpa asked " Granny, how was dad in his childhood?

"Your dad was beautiful from childhood like his dad. One of my aunts in law always said he would be a lady killer in his youth. He was so fair like his dad. When he was little all wanted to adore him taking him in lap. He did not look like my son. I was dark and he was just the opposite. You know, when he was six days old he got very sick. When I took him to the doctor he didn't believe that he was my son. Ha ha ha. Your Dadan always said,' You are lucky to have him as your son '. So Rina came to our house. I was a little bit shocked about how your dad had chosen such a girl who was not so fair, not so tall . Only her eyes were very sharp. So after she was gone his Amma asked him with a laugh ,'Ashish my boy what have you seen in her? You are a great critic of everything. Now what about yourself?" You know what he said?

He said ," Amma,(Ashish called Nipa Amma) I have not seen her outside. I respect her talent. You may not know she is one of the toppers from the girls in our school and her result is so good that all the teachers are proud of her.' Then I only said," If you are happy then we are also happy". But you know which made me think she was different!" Susmita said.

Silpa wanted to know with curiosity," Oh! "What was that surprising thing, Granny "?

" When she first came it was hot. So I went to the kitchen to make lassi(a drink made of curd and sugar, lemon and salt). Rina came to me and started helping me as if she was very much known to me. Then I became her friend. She came to our house very often". Susmita answered.

Silpa asked " Granny, after how many years of their meeting did they get married,"

CHAPTER EIGHT

THE TOUCH OF BREEZE

THE TOUCH OF BREEZE(PART-8)

" Why are you asking all Mithi?(her nickname) I don't know the exact time. What is your plan'!Hun? Susmita asked with smile.

Silpa said ," Granny, you are very naughty! I have curiosity, nothing else. Hey, hey I just passed my class of ten.Only sixteen.

Susmita said ," Well I think after seven or eight years. Then Ashish's granny was alive. She wanted to see Ashish's marriage. After knowing Rina we went to their place to visit. Her parents and elder brother came to our house. So before their wedding, our two families became very close. Very often we met each other on various occasions. We went on a joint trip together. And especially Rina's mom Anamika later became my very close friend. And then after three years Ashish and Rina got married. Ashish was then only 26. Because my mom in law wanted to see her grandson's marriage before death. First two years they stayed in Kolkata. Then Ashish got a big job in Mumbai and they moved there and then your mom also joined a company.You were born in Mumbai".

Silpa Said," Wow! My Granny is great. She is 65 now. But I am sure no one will believe it. You know you are looking like 50 up. Mom also says,' Look at your Granny! How she keeps herself fit at this age. Mom loves you very much.Tell me the secret of your fitness"?

Susmita said with a smile, " Hey listen ,there is no secret! Only every early morning I do exercise or morning walk for thirty minutes. It's my long-term habit. And I don't eat oily and spicy food.

Now tell me how you met Rik?"

Silpa said," Umm! Granny! You are na! Rik is my best friend's Ankita's elder brother. I sometimes go to their house. Rik studies medicine and lives in a hostel.Once he was present on Ankita's birthday. I went there. We saw each other and flirted. It was love at first sight between us. We both smiled to see each other. And then what else! One day he proposed to me with a red rose. I accepted it. You know how romantic he is! He followed me to my tuition center on Valentine's Day. He suddenly stopped me and sat in front of me by kneeling with a red rose. And then said," I love you Sil. Do you have any feelings for me? If yes, then take the rose if no then also take the rose. I will wait then'. You know Granny I didn't tell anyone except you. Ankita also doesn't know".

Susmita," Wow fantastic! So you two kissed each other"? Or did something more?"

" Granny, you are so modern! I just can't imagine. How do you know we kissed? Yes ,we kissed and nothing more. We only chat on the phone. He stays in a hostel.So we can't meet very often like others. But distance doesn't matter in our love". Silpa replied.

In the meantime, Ashish woke up and said, Hey Mom, Silpa, Rina ,come on, get ready! We are near Haridwar. I just saw it on Google Map".

Rina said ," Silpa, take care of Granny. In the time of getting down, catch her hand. The stares are a little high".

" Don't worry mom. Everything will be fine." Silpa answered.

Within half an hour the train stops and all the passengers get down slowly one by another. There was a big statue of Lord Shiva on the outside of the station. Shilpa was very happy to see that. She showed her Granny pointing finger at the statue.

Their car was waiting at the station. They all sat into it and the car started to their hotel. Silpa sat beside Susmita catching her hands. The roads were beautiful and broad. There are lots of hotels all around Haridwar. The city is full of tourists. Lots of foreigners also could be seen.

Susmita told Silpa," You know Mithi (Mithi means sweet) once your Dadan came here and then went to Badrinath. He wanted me to come with him but I didn't listen. Arijit loved to see new places. Before coming anywhere he did research about it. Your Dadan told me, Haridwar is a very ancient holy city and an important Hindu pilgrimage site in Uttarakhand state. The main attraction is the sacred several ghats(bathing steps). Har Ki Pauri is a beautiful ghat where every evening night Ganga Aarti (Ganga river worshiping ceremony) happens. In which tiny flickering lamps are floated on the steps. And after Aarti people also make the tiny lamps float on the river in prayer to God to fulfill their wishes. It is called the Gateway to Gods. And this place is famous for Kumbh Mela which is performed every 12 years. When millions of Hindu devotees gather here. Earlier it was known by the name of Mayapuri for Goddess Maya Devi."

" Really! Granny i, oh my God is that true? Dadan knew a lot. Then we will float diyas(tiny lamps)."

Ashish said ," Yes of course we will. It is very exciting too. But the sad thing is it will only pollute the Ganga river and nothing else".

" Oh! Dad! You always show some scientific reason! I thought to fulfill my wish". Silpa said with a smile.

" Leave your dad, your dad is like that. I am saying your desire must be fulfilled". Rina said with a laugh.Susmita also laughed.

They reached their hotel. It was a three-star hotel. The rooms were very nice, well doctorated and airy. Two rooms were beside one another .One was for Ashish and Rina and another one was for Silpa and Susmita.

Silpa said," Granny , you first go to the washroom. You know I need time. After you are done I will go."

After getting fresh they all sat on the open balcony in front of the rooms. It was a long balcony with a mountain view. Hotel boy served them veg pakora and coffee. Ashish asked him," What is the menu of dinner"? The boy answered," There are rice, dal, potato posto, cauliflower curry, brinjal fry, paneer curry ,chapati, curd chutney, etc. What do you want for dinner mom? I know Ashish will like chapati or paratha.Silpa ,listen I told you before that this zone is totally veg so don't expect chicken or something." Rina said.

Silpa said," Uff! no mom! What do you think of me? I am comfortable with non veg as well as veg. So don't worry. What Granny will eat I will like that. Granny, what do you want for dinner?"

Susmita said with a smile ,"Okay then , my Granny lover asks the boy if he can serve us veg fried rice and paneer butter masala!"

"Yes Granny, we can! Whatever you want, we will make it, don't worry," the boy said."

" Uff! I told you na mom, Granny is too smart. Then we all will eat fried rice and paneer butter masala. Granny ,you are awesome. " Silpa shouted." All laughed loudly.

The next morning after breakfast they went out for sightseeing. Beautiful Haridwar with lots of temples. They visited Chandi Devi Temple, Manasa Devi Temple,Ram Jhula, Lakshman Jhula,Triveni Ghat etc. They went to Rishikesh.This word came from Sanskrit words of Hrishika meaning" senses" and Isha meaning "lord". The name means Lord of the senses. In the name of Hindu God Vishnu. This is called the ' Yoga capital of the world'. They took their lunch in a Bengali restaurant. In the evening they went to Har Ke Pouri Ghat. There were lots of people gathered to see the Arati(Worship God with a big lamp). It was very beautiful. The lamps were floating on the river water. Like small points of light, where they were going no one knew it. Some young men were doing Aarti with large metal diya in their hands.They were following the same steps with the music and Mantra. Silpa began to capture all those moments in her DSLR camera. She was busy with that. Ashish was watching everything standing in one corner. Susmita and Rina floated diyas. Seeing them Silpa also joined them. Susmita prayed to God, folding her palms. Aarti got finished. Ashish took some photos of them on his phone. At that time his phone rang. He called Rina ," Hey your mom is calling. She tried to call you on your phone but it switched off."

Rina said," Wait ,I am coming. My phone has no charge". Rina went to Ashish and they went a little far to hear everything clearly over the phone.She started talking to her mom. Ashish was beside her.

Silpa said," Granny, let me capture some exclusive shots. You sit on the stairs."

Susmita sat there and she felt so calm. Light breeze was coming from the river water and touched her hair and a well known voice was saying to her," How are you my love?" Can you remember me? Or forgotten totally".

Susmita went to her old world leaving everyone in Har Ki Pauri. Her mind was not under her control. As if it just happened a little earlier. Now it is happening with her very often. How much she is gaining her age and that much she could touch her older days. When she stays alone without any work she always remembers her past and she forgets her loneliness.

She saw herself as a little girl with a ponytail who was born and brought up in a village with her little brother in a big joint family with parents, uncles,aunts, grandparents. Her dad was a farmer. There was a small river in front of their house where the village children bathed and caught fish.She and one of her aunt's daughters (Whom she called Dipdi) learnt swimming. In the Autumn Season that river looked beautiful with pink Lotus. Without lotus Durgapuja is not possible. Village boys collected lotus and sold them in the market. She and her Dipdi had a great bonding between them. Dipdi's name was Dipa. And she called her Dipadidi. But in a hurry it became Dipdi. Once Dipa was her best companion.They did everything together like eating meals, taking bath, playing. That time without Dipa, her life was boring.In village Susmita had lots of friends like Dipdi. Parul Anjana ,Sujata, Sulekha with whom she played dolls.(Putul Khela) her granny made dolls with mud for her and Dipa. They dried them in the sun and then decorated those dolls with saree, false jewelry. They arranged the doll's marriage. It was very exciting to them.In the afternoon they all played in a big field. She didn't know where her friends were now! Later she tried to find them from Facebook but couldn't. Susmita had a pet parrot named 'Mithu'. One day when she was in class two, a guy from the neighborhood climbed up their coconut tree (to collect the chicks),where a parrot made a nest and had six baby parrots there. When he got down with those chicks Susmita started crying to get one chick. She told her little aunt ," Choto Pisi (Little aunt) I want one baby ,I want to make it a pet .Please get one from him" .

Her aunt made her understand by saying," O my little Sus Sona, see they are so small. They don't have wings and they can't eat properly. How can you make it a pet?"

" No , no, I want one. I don't want to hear anything ". Saying it she cried more louder . At last they guy gave her one chick.

She and her little aunt put it under a basket to save it from a mole. They fed it milk with the help of a dropper. Within one month its wings showed up and its little body was covered with green feathers.Then her dad bought a cage for Mithu. Its beak was deep red. Susmita gave it a bath under a hand pump. All the time she talked to Mithu. Within a year Mithu learnt to talk . Mithu called her ,'Sus ' and it made Susmita very happy. Mithu liked to eat red chilli and ripe guava very much.

Then Susmita was in class five. It was her exam time so she was studying from morning and then went to school.So Dipa took the cage under the hand pump to give it a bath. Unmindfully she opened the cage. Mithu flew away.

After coming from school when Susmita knew all she got very angry with her Dipdi and said," If I don't get Mithu back I will not eat the whole day. I gave it a bath daily. Nothing happened. And you did one day and made it leave? How careless you are?" Then she quarreled with Dipdi. That was the first and last fighting in between them.

Poor Mithu didn't know how to fly. The crows gathered around it. So in the afternoon it came back and sat on their litchi tree which was in their courtyard. Her middle uncle climbed up the tree with red chili and showed it to Mithu. When it came near to eat he caught it and put it into the cage. Susmita got peace and apologized to

Dipadi.

CHAPTER NINE

THE TOUCH OF BREEZE

THE TOUCH OF BREEZE(PART-9)

Later Mithu could talk like them. It had a black mark around its neck.It loved Susmita very much. She was also crazy for Mithu. Whatever it heard it could say that. Every early morning it said, " Sus get up. It's morning ".

Susmita felt proud to have such a nice parrot in her life as one of her best friends. No friend had a bird like that. Life was so beautiful then. There was not much pressure of education or didn't have any tension.

That time the plague of birds happened. Susmita didn't know anything about it. One day Mithu stopped eating.It was only sleeping . Susmita talked to Mithu but it didn't reply. Generally Mithu always replied. The next early morning Sunmita went to her cage and saw Mithu was sleeping bending its neck one side. She opened the cage. When she touched Mithu she found a very cold hard body. She shouted loudly .Her mom came immediately and understood what happened . Mom hugged her and said," Buri (mom called her Buri), Mithu is no more. Bird doesn't live long my sweetheart. Don't cry. We will buy a new bird, don't worry". That was the first time she touched a dead body and realized sometimes life can also hurt us very hard. This incident she didn't forget ever.

After one year at her class six her parents moved to Kolkata at Jadavpur. After four or five years they sold their village house and lands so all the connections stopped with the village . Lots of times she thought about going there but couldn't. Dipa fled with a boy at a little age and got married. Susmita and Dipa were very close to each other.They promised never to get apart. Then after the birth of her second daughter she died due to blood cancer.

That time Susmita was in Kolkata busy with studying. So she could not see her Dipadi at her last time. It hurts her very much.Their promise only became a word. Now memorizing Dipadi her heart becomes heavy.

Coming to Kolkata she got another group of friends. In her class eleven she met a new girl whose name was Paromita. She was tall ,fair and beautiful and could sing very well. Susmita and Paromita became best friends within a few days. Susmita called her you are my 'opermita'(oper means opposite side, mita means friend). They were so close in school they sat together. Shared tiffin and all the time stuck together. School teachers called themSusmita and Paromita, 'Manik jod (Ruby joint). Paromita was a very good student.

One day Paromita told her," Susmita you know, I like a guy whose name is Fahim.We both learn spoken English at the same institution.When he looks at me I forget my world and my world gets fed. He is Muslim. So sometimes I think ,why was I born as Hindu ? Why do people hate another religion? He wrote me a love letter where he said he would fight to value our love till the end .But I am not so brave to accept his love."

Susmita was surprised to know all. Later she knew that Paromita's dad threatened Fahim not to try to keep any relation with Paromita. Paromita cried a lot after coming to school and Promised she would never forget Fahim and would never get married with anyone. In class twelve she got poor marks .After that they got distracted by each other. They got admission to different colleges.That time there was no mobile phone so ultimately Susmita didn't know how Paromtia was then?" Later she learned from one old friend that Paromita went to Australia with her husband .

"Granny ,look at me . Where have you lost your mind? You are looking so beautiful I wanna capture this time. Let's click some of your photos" Shilpa cried out.

Susmita's mind came back to Har Ki Pauri ghat again. She was embarrassed. And said," Sorry Mithi my darling, I was thinking something. Aree don't take my photo. I am getting old".

" Oh! Granny, you are my sweet honey. You look wonderful in white saree. Do you know how gorgeous you are looking ? So keep silent only do what I am saying ". Silpa said in a loud voice.

She took lots of photos. Then they visited Haridwar market. The woolen material, shawl, and blanket were cheap there. Rina bought lots of things. Ashish said," Who will carry your luggage? Don't make it too heavy please. We can get everything in our market also."

Rina answered,"Aree , what are you saying? I have to give gifts to my friends. Don't worry I will carry my luggage"! Susmita bought sweaters for Ashish, Rina and Silpa. Rina chose a beautiful white shawl for Susmita. Though Susmita opposed it, no one heard it so she had to take it.

After coming to the hotel they had their dinner and fell asleep quickly because they all were tired.

The next morning they started their journey to Harsil by car. It is a village situated on the banks of river Bhagirathi. It is a romantic place of Garhwal. In the 1815 Anglo- Nepal war, British raj sided with the kingdom of Garwal and as a reward they were given the eastern half of Garhwal. On the way they got to a place named Uttarkashi which is very beautiful. They stopped there for tea .It was a small city. The roads were well planned. There were electric lights on both sides of the roads. There were lots of small and big hotels.The scenic beauty was wonderful. Silpa became so excited so she opened her camera and filmed everything. Her mom said, "Silpa now stops. Let's sit in the car and we have to go to Harshil".

"Mom, please give me a few more times. Granny see! What a beautiful and big flower on that tree. This must be a hilly flower. I have not seen it ever. I have to take a shot of it ". She shouted.

The hilly roads of Harshil were not so broad. The driver showed them a broken car beside one point of the road and said there was an accident that happened a few months ago.

On the way Ashish asked, "Silpa, do you know which Indian film maker made this hilly village famous?"

" Oh really. I don't know anything dad. Why didn't you tell me before? I will google it." Silpa replied.

" Though this village has a beautiful ancient story. According to local lore, there was a British settler named Fredric E Wilson who introduced this area for the first time. He fell in love with Harshil and a local girl. He made this place his home.He introduced apple cultivation here and changed its economy. Now this place is famous for various apple production. Now tell me the name of the Indian film maker"? Ashish said

" Mithi see! Your dad has the same habit as your Dadan. He also likes to research everything before going for a tour, " Susmita said while laughing.

Silpa said,"Oh dad! I don't know. Okay just wait a few. Let me Google it. Oh shit! there is no signal on my phone." .

Rina smiled and said," This is a new craze of young people. Whatever they want to know, they will search it from Google. And no doubt it's really helpful."

Silpa became impatient to know the name. Then Susmita said," Oh my little Silpa, I am telling you. There was a famous Hindi filmmaker named Raj Kapur. He was also a great actor. He made a Hindi movie and it became a superhit. It was ,'Ram Teri Ganga Maili'. This man first time got attracted to the beauty of it. And did the shooting of his movie here. People used to know about it. From then on, tourists started coming here".

" Oh my God! Granny ,how do you know everything? I already started loving this place". Silpa said.

" Once your Dadan planned to come here by reading about this place from a Bengali magazine Sananda. He planned to visit here but it didn't happen". Susmita replied.

Then they reached Harsil. It was a small hilly village. From the road they saw the plants holding some red flowers or fruits. Susmita asked a local guy," What are these"? The guy answered very casually," These are apples mam."

After getting down from the car they entered their hotel. It was nice. There was a big ground in front of the hotel. And there were many apple trees around the hotel. After getting fresh they took their veg lunch with dal,rice, aloo jeera, paneer chutney, papad and curd. It was also a veg zone. After taking some rest in the afternoon they all went to visit the place around there on foot. It was a very calm and quiet place.There was a bridge over a river. When they reached that bridge the sunlight was low. The light touched the water and it was reflecting on it. Silpa was trying to catch the moments in her camera. Ashish was doing the video of water going with a cool noise on his Iphone.

Susmita said to Rina," Do you know Rina ,why is this bridge so famous?" Hearing it, Silpa asked " Really is it a famous bridge! Why Granny?"

" This is the bridge where the heroine of the movie Mandakini waited to meet the hero". Susmita said with a smile.

" O! That's it ! Wow, very interesting. After going back I will certainly see the movie from youtube,'Ram Teri Ganga Maili ' . Is that the name of the movie ,right Granny ? Silpa asked.

She captured lots of photos. She shouted," Mom dad ,come here stand in a romantic mood. I have to take yours together. And then dad you will take me,mom and Granny together. She took lots of selfies on her phone.

Then they saw the post office made of wood. From where the heroine of the movie went to collect letters sent by the hero. First time Silpa saw a village post office in her life. So she was just astonished to see it. She hugged Ashish and said," Thank you dad. For your super trip.I will really gonna miss it if I didn't come".

Ashish smiled and said," Okay,darling. If you are happy then I also feel delighted. There is nothing in my life except making you happy."

Then they entered an apple orchard. It was a very large area.There were lots of apple trees full of apples. It was the end of September so apples started to ripe.There were lots of apples that had fallen on the ground.All were very happy to see it.

There was a military camp of Indian soldiers. When they went there a young military man came to them hearing their Bengali language. He was also a Bengali.He held his palms together and said to them," Namaste.I am Tarun from Bankura.You are Bengali. I understood after listening to your language. I joined the military at the age of 23. I have my family with two kids and parents.They live in Bankura. I am tired of not speaking in Bengali for a long time. Here no one understands Bengali. The feeling of talking to our own mother tongue is different. You come here for a tour? Will you mind if I want to join you? Don't worry I will show you the whole military camp."

Ashish showed him namaste and said,'' Hey, no no why do we mind? It's our pleasure. Meet my wife Rina, daughter Silpa and mom". All said him namaste with folding their palms.

Suddenly Tarun looked at Susmita and said to her," Mam, I think you are very well known to me. In my off time I like to read story books. It is my passion.I have read the novel 'Shade' .There I saw the author's photo. She was like you.That book brought tears to my eyes. It was such a beautiful book. And the story just touched my heart. I know in the kolkata book fair most of the authors get together. So I wanted to meet the author.If you don't mind, are you that author mam?"

Susmita said,"Oh yes ! You are right.Thanks a lot for your appreciation .And I am feeling honored to hear your words."

" Mam, what are you saying! I am overwhelmed ! May I get your autograph please." Saying it he spread his pocket diary. Susmita gave her autograph.

Tarun said ," Today it will be my pleasure to become your tourist guide. If you agree, then let me show you our military kingdom".

Silpa said ," Why not .We will be very glad".

First he took them to the military camp. It was a very large area. There were so many small tents where the military man stayed and very big trucks also. They used to know that with those trucks military men go to different places . Taking pictures was prohibited there. So Silpa couldn't take a single photo. She became a little upset. Tarun fed them tea from the camp.

They knew about camouflage trees and military uniforms.Tarun said to them,"Military uses camouflage to hide them from the enemy. The main objective of military camouflage is to deceive the enemy as to the presence, position and intentions of military formations." Then Tarun took them to a big apple orchard.There were many types of apples grown there like red, green, white etc.

CHAPTER TEN

THE TOUCH OF BREEZE

THE TOUCH OF BREEZE(PART-10)

That zone is famous for red apples . There were lots of apples that had fallen on the ground. Silpa whispered to Susmita's ear," Granny,look how many apples. I am greedy to take some". Tarun heard it and said," Hey, don't worry! . I am here in your services madam! Pluck from the tree fresh apples as much as you wish. But don't take them from the ground.All are rotten."

Ashish said ," No ,no what are you saying? The orchard owner can mind something"?. " Sir, this is Umar uncle's garden. He is a local farmer. You may not know that the orchard owner sold the garden to the big business man of Uttarkashi, when just the apple flowers bloomed.So now they are only the guard.They have no right on the apples. So don't worry Silpa. Here I am the guarantor." Tarun said with a Laugh.

Silpa and Rina plucked some apples. Both were extremely happy because it was the first time they got a chance to pluck apples from trees.Tarun plucked some apples and gave them to Susmita. Then Tarun showed them the fields where various types of beans were grown.The green valley was very attractive for beans! Susmita and Silpa plucked some white beans from the field.They thanked Tarun for showing them beautiful Harsil. Tarun and Ashish exchanged their phone numbers.Tarun was also very happy to get a Bengali family and especially meet with Susmita.

After finishing dinner, they went to their room. Silpa showed Susmita all the photos from the camera and said," Granny , tell me how I am as a photographer ?" Susmita laughed and replied," I know my Silpa is the number one not only as a photographer but in all fields."

In the hilly regions people get to sleep very early. While sleeping at 9p.m on the bed Silpa said," Granny, I can't sleep so soon and here the internet is very slow. So please tell me about your village .You know I am very curious to know all. Granny , please tell me.``

Susmita said," Okay, okay.I am gonna tell you. My village was situated in North 24 pgs. It is a plain land by the river side.Most of the people had a big garden in front of their house. Mostly they were farmers.And there were lots of fruit trees in the garden. My dad also had the same. Most of the houses were made of mud. Brick houses were rare. We had mango trees, jack fruit trees, berry trees, coconut trees ,litchi trees, lemon trees and so on. We didn't need to buy fruits from the market except the fruits from hilly areas. Most of the families had cows. So we could drink pure cow milk. There was no electricity in our village.The weather was not so hot like now. Houses were surrounded by trees so Summer was not so painful. Now you can't stay without A.C but at that time we didn't know what AC was? We studied in the light of kerosene oil. Our school was a free primary school where no proper sitting arrangement was done. From childhood we learnt how to keep toleration. In the Summer season there was a wind blowing in the afternoon which was called Kalbaishaki. The raw mangoes dropped down and all the village children gathered under the mango tree to pick them. It was so exhilarating to us you just can't imagine. My granny made various kinds of mango pickles with them. They were so delicious! Now my mouth is also watered. Sometimes we siblings ate pickles by stealing secretly."

"Really Granny! Iss! You were so lucky. Then tell me next". "Then if our Granny could understand it then she scolded us with love and said,' Aree I will not eat. These are for you. When there would be no mangoes but you wanted to eat mango then you could eat.' You know then the roads were also muddy. In the rainy season the roads were full of mud so there was a big problem in communication. There was only a two-day market in a week (Thursday and Sunday) , not all the days like now. People from near the villages came to that market to buy or sell. We only ate fish two or three days a week. Most of the families had their own pond where they reared fish. If any guest came or for some occasions like marriage, rice ceremony then they were caught. Fish and rice are the favorite meals of Bengali people." Susmita said.

" Granny , mom and dad are also Bengali but I don't think they love fish so much". Silpa asked.

" Yes,you are right ,their habit has been changed by staying outside of Bengal so long. You know, in my childhood if we got fish in meals we ate more than other days. There was a small river in our village. We all bathed there. While bathing in the river the village children often caught small fish with Gamcha.(The cloth used for drying the body).I had a cousin sister Dipadidi. She and I caught lots of fish.You know Mithi , in Autumn season Bengali people celebrate Durga puja. There was only one Puja arranged in our village.In the open field of that market. Not so much puja like now in Kolkata. We got only one new frock at that time. And I wore that frock for four days of puja.In the evening we went to see puja with my aunt. There was a fair on that ground due to puja. From there we ate sweets or colored ice cream. There were no sweets shops near our house.So we were greedy for sweets. If any guests came then they were served the coconut sweets made by my Granny. Susmita said.

" Wow Granny , that's fantastic. Tell me something about village love". Silpa said.

" That time phones were not available. Young boys and girls wrote love letters to express their love. As now you chat over the phone like that!" Susmita said with a laugh.

" Accha Granny , have you ever written a love letter to any boy"? Silpa asked with a mischievous smile.

" No darling, I didn't get a chance to write it. Because I came here to Kolkata after passing class five. And frankly speaking we were not so smart like the children of now. But I wrote love letters for others. I was good at studying and my handwriting was very good. So my Dipadi requested me to write love letters for her boyfriend. I wrote whatever she said. I got a love letter from someone ". Susmita replied.

" Really ,Granny! I am excited to know it, ".Silpa said.

" You are so naughty. You only want to hear my love story. There was a boy living next door to us named Utpal. He was three years older than me. But dropped one year in class.We played together. In primary school we went together. When my dad announced that we are leaving our village permanently. Because that time plowing was not profitable. One or two months before coming to Kolkata(I can't remember now).One afternoon when we went to play in the field Utpal handed a piece of paper and said ,' This is only for you. Don't show anyone. After reaching home, read it and write the answer to me.' I was too afraid. I had a fear in my mind that if anyone could see this what would happen? But I was also excited to read it. So while doing homework in the evening I opened the paper. He wrote,' My dear Susmita, don't leave me alone. I love you very much. I can't live without you. When we grow up I will be your husband. And you will be my wife. Make your dad understand no to go anywhere. I love you ,I love you, I love you, I love you, I love you, people say if we say anything five times then it happens in our life. Write your answer. I will wait for it'. Your's Utpal. Reading the letter I was sweating.My body was shaking. It was my first love letter. I never thought of Utpal in this way. Most of the spelling was incorrect. I tore out the paper into very small pieces so that no one could read it. Then I threw it into our pond. I didn't reply.Then I didn't know what happened to me! After that incident I felt very shy to look at him. And then we came to Kolkata and slowly I got busy with my study and forgot everything. And those days became sweet memories in my life. Silpa, my sweetheart, I am feeling very sleepy. I will tell you later." Susmita said.

" Okay, Granny thank you, it was so sweet, let's sleep. Tomorrow we have to wake up early . Good night."Saying it, Silpa switches off the light.

The next morning after having breakfast they went to see the top four beautiful spots of Harsil by car.At first they visited Dharali. It was a beautiful place three km from Harsil. The natural beauty was just gorgeous.The weather was soothing, not so cold. Rina brought some hot tea in a flax from the hotel. She offered it to everyone. But Susmita doesn't like too much tea. So she refused. But Ashish likes tea the most as his dad. So he took a cup. Silpa was busy with her camera. This place reminded her about Arijit. Who loved to see hills.

After that they went to another village. Its name was Mukhwas. It is one of the popular tourist attractions of Harsil just one K.m away.This place is called the winter home of Goddess Gangotree. In the winter the heavy snow makes this place like heaven. Everything around was clean. As if someone had made it beautiful with the touch of a magical stick. Light breeze and the green nature made the environment unique. Silpa requested everyone to stand together and the driver took their photo.

Their next journey was Sattal. It is a group of seven freshwater lakes with nature's bounty and loads of migratory birds and panoramic vistas. This place is awesome. It is situated in Kumaon Region at an elevation of 1370m above sea level and boasts of its cluster seven lakes. All were feeling cold. So they wore jackets and Susmita took her shawl.

Ashish shouted," Mom wrap it well."

" Ok, Don't worry ,a hilly cold is not harmful for me.You know your dad took me to so many hilly regions during the full winter." Susmita replied. " I know mom, but then you were young. Though you are not old enough now ,just be careful " . Ashish said with a laugh.

Ashish asked Rina," Do you know the name of seven lakes? I really don't know . Do you have any idea?"

Rina answered," Ei, nah! Do I analyze like you? Or I don't search Google like Silpa. But I guess mom can know! Mom, do you know the names?"

"Umm, no I never heard. In fact I didn't know that there were such lakes here. I want to know the name. Mithi, ask your Google! Let's see if it can help us or not"! Susmita said.

" Sorry Granny , my net connection is slow. Without the net my google is like a powerless Alien. Dad, I also want to know names." Silpa shouted and laughed.

The driver was a local guy. Hearing all he said,"Sir, I know the name of the lakes. All are beautiful names. They are Ram, Sita, Lakshman, Bharat all are related to Ramayana and the rest are Panna, Naldaymanti Tal and SukhaTal and all are interconnected to each other".

" Wow, great. Silpa, memorese all. " Ashish said.

This area was covered by oaks and pine trees. There was fresh green all around to satisfy the mind. And the cold air was coming from the lake. Ashish and Rina took another cup of tea, this time Susmita also joined them. Rina gave everyone pieces of cake with tea. The driver also drank tea.

Silpa didn't eat cake, she opened a packet of potato chips and started eating.

The cool air touched the heart of Sumita and one name came to her mind that was her Breeze,her secret love.She hid him in her heart from everyone till then.

Ashish said," Let's go to the next spot. There we will take our lunch. Silpa, now stop your camera. Rina please come and sit in the car. Mom,what are you thinking! Let's go".

"Oh yes ,I am coming". Saying this, Susmita sat in the car.

When everyone sat in the car and it started running.

They reached the next spot, Gangnani. It was twenty six km before Harshil. This place is mostly famous for its hot water spring.This place is a perfect view for pictures. With the sunlight it was looking great. Scenic beauty was superb. Hills were all around. The roads were zigzagging. There was a big hotel where they took their lunch.

They came back in the afternoon. After taking some rest all came to the lawn in their hotel. There were some other tourists also present. There were a few chairs where Susmita, Ashish, Rina sat and started talking together. One of her friends called Silpa over the phone so she got busy with talking.

Susmita said ," Ashish, after going back to Jadavpur I have to repair my washing machine. Otherwise it will be a problem". " Listen ! Mom, I will do it. You don't worry. We will go back to Mumbai after staying two days with you. And you are also going with us to Mumbai. You will come back after Diwali.(It is a festival of victory of good over evil) .This time we will celebrate Diwali together in Mumbai."Ashish said.

" Yes mom, you have to go. Diwali is very famous in Mumbai. Silpa will be very happy to get you. Please don't say no." Rina said.

There was a recently married couple. The girl asked Susmita" Are you from Jadavpur aunty? I am from Dhakuria. Just a neighbor of yours".

" Oh! That's it! Bah! Very good! What is your name?" Susmita asked.

CHAPTER ELEVEN

THE TOUCH OF BREEZE

THE TOUCH OF BREEZE(PART-11)

" I am Sweta Chatterjee and he is my husband Kiran Aher from Maharashtra. We got married six months earlier". She said,

" Oh! You meet my son Ashish, my daughter in law Rina and there is my granddaughter Silpa. They also live in Mumbai" Susmita replied.

Kiran folded his palms and said to everyone, "Namaste". They also did the same.

Then they started talking. Hotel served them tea and Potato pakora.

Susmita asked Sweta , "Do you know about Binodini girls school! There I studied".

" Oh ! That is beside our house. Then you must know Babubagan, famous for Durga puja". Sweta asked .

"I know Babubagan very well. You know which day our school declared the puja holiday, we friends went to see the Babubagan's puja in a group.That day we got half day of school. And all the students were allowed to wear new dress, not school uniform. We had lots of fun while going there." Susmita answered with a smile.

In the meantime Silpa finished talking and sat beside Susmita.Rina said to her," Silpa see, your Granny has got a neighbor. She is Sweta and he is her husband Kiran."

"Wow, that is good! I see my Granny is too famous. Look Granny! Here you have got your neighbor also." Silpa hugged Susmita with a smile.

" So Kiran, how is Sweta ? Is she fit for your culture? How did you meet?" Susmita asked.

Kiran answered," Yes ,she is trying to acquire our culture. At first my mom and dad didn't want her in our family but now they love her very much. And Sweta is very good and in my opinion Bengali women are very adjustable. Ha ha, don't think I am trying to impress you Sweta ." Kiran said with a smile looking at her.

Sweta said," My office was in Kolkata. Once they transferred me to Pune for six months for training. There Kiran was our project leader. From there we knew each other. He liked me. I didn't think he loved me. One day there was a Ganesh Puja at his home so he invited me and told me to wear a saree. I went there. I touched his parents feet to take blessings. His mom,dad and other family members were very interested in me. They asked me lots of things about my family, parents. I was thinking about what was going on there?; After that I knew the whole mystery ".

" Oh! Was there any mystery?" Rina asked.

Kiran said," Actually, In our family and culture, arranged marriage is more acceptable than love marriage.Not like Kolkata,Kolkata is very modern in this aspect. Even now before marriage our family looks after the farming lands of the bride or groom's dad .I fell in love with her but I knew my dad would not take it easily. They didn't know anything about Bengali culture. So before her visit to our house I told everything about her to my mom. I requested mom to make my dad and other family members understand and did a little bit of advertisement about Sweta . I knew that after seeing her everyone would like her. And you know! I didn't want to lose her. I just loved her so much . I knew from her that She had no affair. So that was the mystery, all my family members were trying to know about her that day.After talking to Sweta my mom was very much happy. My dad had some objections but after talking to her parents he slowly changed his mind. After getting the green signal from my mom.I proposed to her. And I guess she was ready to accept it. Am I right na Sweta?" telling it Kiran smiled.

" What should I do? If a handsome man proposed to me in front of all the office staff,' I love you Sweta'. I have to take it na "! My dad was very much worried! Because we also didn't have any idea about Marathi people. I first told about Kiran to my Bordi (Eldest sister). And she told my parents.That Kiran is a very good guy. Then my dad talked over the phone with Kiran. And then with his dad. His dad invited my parents to their place. After that my parents , my bordi and Jiju(husband of elder sister) came to their house. Kiran's family also came to Kolkata and then everything happened smoothly. We got married in Kolkata in Bengali culture and then in Mumbai in Marathi culture. After marriage I came to his house. As we are working in the same office. First few days I was very nervous about how to manage everything. Kiran taught me a few Marathi recipes and I cooked and served them and all were praised. Especially my mom in law. Then I tried some Bengali recipes. And ultimately I realized if you cook well and can smile you can conquer everything. It is right na aunty?" My mom in law is now my best friend. But I am still learning their various types of puja." Sweta replied.

Susmita said ," You are right Sweta , a smiling face can win it all".

" Wow ! What a fantastic love story ! I am just thrilled to hear all about it. Let's take a group photo. Silpa shouted.

All laughed and Susmita said," May God keep your love happy forever". "Thank you so much mam! Have a great tour". Kiran replied.

It was became dark and cold winds were blowing. So they left the lawn saying everyone good night and went to their hotel room. The stars were glowing in the clear sky. Susmita looked outside from the window. The valley was looking like a land of thousand diyas(lamps) as everywhere the electric lamps were showing like points of light in the dark. Susmita always loves this beauty of hills very much. At night they finished their dinner with paratha and Rajma curry. The hotel served them very tasty delicious apples. It was their rule to serve the guests a special apple last night at the hotel. The pieces were just melting into the mouth. It was also their last night In Harsil.

At night sleeping on bed Silpa asked Susmita, "Granny , when did you fall in love for the first time ? Tell me about your teenage love. Please ".

" Uff ! You got me again. You are running after my love story ". Susmita replied with smile.

" No , no Granny ,please tell, I can't sleep so early". Silpa requested.

" Okay, my honey,when I was in class eight I took admission in a tuition center. Far from our house. My uncle used to take me there. There studied a boy whose name was Srijit. He was very tall and handsome. I was good at English so my teacher liked me very much. Srjit was also very good at English. So our teacher made two groups with the students. One was good, another was weak students. I and Srijit were in the same team. He sat beside me. And I could understand that very often he looked at me in a romantic mood. I felt very shy to look at him in this way. I felt happy from the bottom of my heart. His house was just near the center. So he reached home quickly after finishing class he stood at the balcony only to see me. One day it was Saraswati puja. You know Devi Saraswati is the Goddess of education and creativity. And for Bengali young people that day is called Bengali Valentine 's day.That day is the total holiday from study. Saraswati puja was also held in our tuition center. I didn't get time the whole day to go there. Our teacher requested everyone to go there in the evening. Because dinner was arranged there with fried rice, dum aloo,jajuba chutney, papad and rasgulla. I went there wearing a yellow saree.And I was looking like a lady. That was the first time I wore a saree. Though my mom taught me to manage it. Srijit was looking at me continuously. He wore a white Kurta and Pajamas.He looked very mature. After finishing dinner when I was washing my hands he came close to me and whispered in my air," Susmita, I love you. From the first day I fell in love with you. The whole day you come to my mind. I don't know what you think about me.So many girls study here but you are special and you always attract me. Please try to understand."

" Wow! Granny ! Srijit was So romantic! You must accept his love! Right !" Silpa said with a smile.

" I couldn't say anything then. My dad was very strict at that time and I was busy with studying. So I ignored him. Basically I stopped talking to him . I don't know what happened to me.Why did I behave like this? I liked him very much. Maybe I didn't understand what love is ? Or maybe I was stupid not so smart like a city girl. He tried many ways to impress me. That I enjoyed a lot. I didn't value him. After two years we passed class ten and left the coaching center.At the last day I said to him ,"Srijit, I am sorry." That was the last day we talked to each other. Then I missed him. But there was no contact between us. After six or seven months , I saw him with a girl catching each other's hands, out of the bus window while going somewhere. He also saw me. That day I wanted to talk to him.He ignored me.My tears came. I don't know why? That was the end of my teenage love story." Susmita said.

Oh ! Granny how unromantic you are ! I thought something would happen in between you and him but you spoiled everything. Why didn't you accept his love?Hun! I thought you would kiss him. What a boring story? If I was in your place I would love to accept immediately .You are hiding something. I gotta sleep". Silpa said with fake anger.

"Hey ,no, my sweetheart, I have nothing to hide from you. I was then only 15 years and so many years ago falling in love with someone was very shameful in Bengali culture. And especially those families who were conservative for them, kissing was just a nightmare. Before doing anything we had to think about everything so that our parents didn't feel ashamed of our behavior. I was not so smart like you and our life was not so luxurious, my dad was fighting financially with his new factory in Kolkata.And we all were very worried about it. So I had a goal to do something good in life. And you can say I became smart and I knew what love is after marrying your Dadan. Did you understand my Mithi Sona? Okay good night". Susmita said.

The next morning they started for Gongothri . It took only one hour by car. The road was extremely steep. Greenaries were all around. How high they were going, the weather was cooling more. Silpa sat tightly with Susmita. She was doing a video of the beauty. On the way Ashish said," You know Mithi, Gangothri means sacred river of India and it is situated in Uttarakhand it is an important pilgrimage for Hindus. It is at a height of 3100 meters."

" Oh! So high!" Rina said in surprise.

Ashish said, "Hum! Right! There is the temple of Goddess Ganga and it is one of the highest temples. According to Hindu legend, Goddess Ganga descended here when Lord Shiva released the mighty river from the locks of his hair. The holy River Ganga originates from the Gangotri glacier, located here, and is called Bhagirathi. But people said it came from Lord Shiva".

" I knew my dad would show the scientific reason" Silpa laughed and said.

Ashish continued", This Gangotri temple was built by Gorkha General Amar Singh Thapa, in the 18th century and is situated on the left bank of Bhagirathi river. The temple is nested amidst the beautiful surroundings of deodars and pine trees. Gangotri Glacier originates at the northern pole of the Chaukhamba mountain range.The terminus of the glacier is Gaumukh .Tourists love to enjoy trekking to Gaumukh. Another beautiful trekking point is Tapovan Trek. It's a beautiful place. Another beautiful trekking place is Kedartal though trekking is very difficult here but the route has stunning views of snow clad mountains.That reduces the pain of trekking."

" Well, dad ,we are going trekking na! I wanna go there. I don't mind suffering." Silpa said with great interest.

"Yes we should go. After coming so far, if we don't go to Gomukh then it would be a regret.And my friends said Tapovan is just unique. So be ready ". Ashish answered.

" Granny , what are you gonna do! You are going na"! Silpa asked Susmita.

" Am I mad! What are you saying? If I go, all will stop going and will look at me! Do you want that?" Susmita said mischievously.

" Silpa, Granny can't go there. She will not have this tough journey at this age. And I will stay at the hotel. I don't think I will be able to go. Your dad and you will enjoy it." Rina said in worry.

" Hey, no you have to go. Otherwise we will not go.Why you will not do it! You must go.I had planned this tour only for it. Now don't say it like this. It will upset me, please." Ashish said with a request.

Susmia said," Babu,(Ashish's nickname) ,don't worry. Rina will go. She is joking! That's right! Rina?"

In the meantime their car stopped in front of a nice hotel. They all entered into it. The rooms were on the first floor. Hotel boy took their bags into their room. At the reception Ashish finished some formality. From the hotel they got tea, bread with butter and a kind of laddu. Rina and Susmita took only tea. Because they wanted to worship Goddess Ganga while fasting. After breakfast they went to Gangotri Temple by foot.

CHAPTER TWELVE

THE TOUCH OF BREEZE

THE TOUCH OF BREEZE(PART-12)

It was near their hotel. There were lots of big and small hotels beside the road. There were houses of the local people.Their earnings depend on Apple business and tourism. There were lots of small shops around the temple.From one shop they took the necessary things to worship the Goddess Ganga. So many people gathered there. All stood by putting their palms together. The priest, chanting mantras. Then he said to everyone to wish for something from Mother Ganga .

Silpa whispered to Susmita," Granny! What are you wishing for? I am watching you just get lost from this world."

Susmita felt a little embarrassed and said," No! Bap! I was praying for everyone's good. Nothing else my dear. Tell me what you have wished for. When you will see Rik! That is ?".

" Uff Granny , I can see him whenever I want by video call. Time has changed Granny. I was praying for our successful Gaumukh trekking." Silpa replied.

Then they visited the nearby place there.So many foreigners also came. It was too cold so Ashis, Rina and Susmita decided to take tea from a nearby shop. Silpa doesn't like tea too much. So she was looking around and clicking her camera.

Rina and Susmita felt hungry so they ordered for Aloo Paratha. Meanwhile They saw Silpa had met a foreign couple and was talking to them. After finishing everything they return back to their hotel.

After lunch and taking a little rest they went to roam around the nearby place of Gangotri.There was a beautiful place with some chairs, on which tourists can sit and enjoy the mountain view. They sat there.

Silpa said, " You know dad, the couple whom I met at noon was from America. Then they were coming after trekking from Gaumukh. I realized as I saw their rucksacks on their backs. So I introduced myself and talked to them. Granny , you know I didn't feel American English was too tough.The lady was Camilla and her partner was Zac. They came here for a trip . Mom, you saw how fair they were! I took a few selfies with them. I would like to show my friends. I asked Camilla about their experience of going to Gaumukh and Tapovan. Because tomorrow we have a plan for it. Camilla said," It's a wonderful experience. The beauty of the route can't be expressed by words. And reaching there we felt like we entered heaven. Though the trekking journey was a little tough. We enjoyed it a lot. We couldn't imagine India has such a unique place on which anyone can feel proud ". I got relaxed by listening to them.I knew all the information of the journey and I am excited to do my first trekking with my parents."

" Wow! Mithi you learnt how to rescherce like your dad! It is called gene!" Susmita said with a smile.

" Granny ! You are so smart! Do you know mom, Camilla is a very good girl. She became almost my friend. She invited me to visit her city New York and told me so many things about her.You can't imagine her partner Zac staying together for the last three years without marrying. She is now twenty. Can you imagine it here? If I am a little late coming from tuition at night. You know Granny ,how many times does mom make phone calls ? Their life is totally different from ours! They are free to do everything. They don't have any boundaries to stay with their parents. How beautiful is their life ? Right dad"? Silpa said.

Ashish answered," Yes you are right, their life is different but Mithi we have a family bonding which is very important in life.Yes they are free to do all that's why they don't compromise with anything.They are self sufficient so they can divorce or break any relationship at any time without thinking about children or society.We always think about the sentiment of others. I am not saying that all the time it's good to hear after society but sometimes it's necessary to keep a family tight.Otherwise our children will be the most sufferer. Now you think you came here with Granny didn't you feel good! This is called family bonding.You know my mom is my inspiration. She taught me how to keep patience! In the world I respect her most. Only because of her right decision ,I got my Amma's love and a family. I think our Indian culture values the people . It is important to family bonding. Sometimes it may be very painful to adjust with everything.My mom did it. For that reason my mom is the best``.Saying that he hugged Susmita.

Rina asked," Tell me Shilpa, don't you feel good when I call you over the phone? I didn't know it. Your dad is a man. So your Granny never stopped Ashish from doing anything. You are a girl so I feel worried about you. Nothing else".

" Okay Mom sorry! I understood the cultural difference between our India and them. But ultimately we have to live happily. If people feel happy with their culture then it's good. Am I right dad? Let's go! Tomorrow we have to wake up early, "Silpa said.

" Yes my Mithi ,darling. You are totally right. Whatever our culture is, at the end we all need to be happy with life. We all have the right to get everything in life. Maybe it is Indian or American. Life is precious. So we all have to live it fully." Ashish said.

In the evening. The Arti was going on with a large lamp. The bell of the temple rang loudly. They spent a few times there and then came back to the hotel.

Ashish said," Listen , I have to go to reception because of some formality for Goumukh trekking. We need to submit a voter I card , photos and the necessary papers. So you people continue to chat. I am coming back.," Rina said," I will go with you".They both went to reception.

After they went Silpa asked," Granny! you saw, how much dad loves you! Actually you always supported dad. You were never opposed to him. Is that right Granny?

Susmita replied," Yes Mithi, you are right. I never interfere in his life. I believe in freedom. I don't think we can get something by force. Especially love. The first time Ashish went for a tour with Rina before marriage I didn't say anything but his Amma opposed it a lot .I always wanted to see him happy because he also suffered a lot for our fighting. After your Dadan's gone I realized,as an educated woman, I did wrong. Though from my childhood I had lots of patience. But all the time I couldn't maintain it. That doesn't mean we had no love in between us. Only we had different views."

While saying Susmita's eyes filled with tears. Seeing that Silpa said, " Granny, ,please. Dad always says,' I never saw so much patience in a woman like my mom.' So don't regret it. Just enjoy the trip. Now listen to my problem. I love my mom's care but sometimes I feel a little disgusting. Mom can't understand I am a grown up lady".

" Ok! I will talk to Rina. But moms are like that.My mom was also the same. She always told me not to be friends with boys. You see na that's why my teenage love got messed up. I always listened to my parents. Rina does not allow you to talk to Rik?" Saying that,Susmita smiled a little.

" Granny , you know my friends sometimes go to a party in a nightclub but mom never allowed me to go there. Mom doesn't like my staying outside long. You know, before Zac, Camilla had another boyfriend. My two friends already had sex with their boyfriends . If mom hears it I don't know what she will do?Tell me Granny when you have sex first time!" Silpa asked.

" Ei what are you asking me? Don't you feel shy to ask such questions "? Susmita laughed and said.

" Oh! Granny I am a grown up lady.This is the problem of Indian culture. They don't discuss everything with children.That's why teasing, rape etc happens. I think if we can see boys and girls in the same way and can think sex is an important part of life and can make the young people understand the good or evil part of it then our society will develop more. My Granny is too smart and she is a great writer. And you are one of my best friend so I am curious about you.Tell me na Nani please ". Silpa said

" Well I had first time sex with your Dadan after marriage." Susmita said.

" Granny, you had arranged marriage. How could you do it with a stranger like Dadan? I just can't imagine that two unknown people can do sex easily ". Silpa asked.

" Yes you can say it. Do you know there is a special night for newly married couples? Bengali people call it Fullsajja or Suhagrat ,and that night is their first sex night. I and your Dadan did not do anything that night. Because I was scared. I didn't know him a little. So Dadan first few nights talked to me about my life and made myself comfortable with him and then after fifteen or sixteen days when we became known to each other then he bought flowers and spread them on the bed. My first sex was a little painful. I was bleeded. Then your Dadan became afraid because it was also his first sex. He wanted to call his mom to take me to a doctor. I was so shy, I told him not to be worried and to wait for the next day.Next two days we did nothing and then it became normal. That time I fell in love with your Dadan madly. But then after a few years our life became a little difficult and we lost the essence of love. I never thought to divorce him or make your dad apart from him or his Amma or his dad. I became an earning machine. My tears were then my companion. Your Dadan had stopped working.His medicines were very costly. Your dad was studying. So all the expenses came over me. Very often we had fights. And I didn't sleep with him when we quarreled. A hatred came to mind about my life and about men and him. I tried to adjust with everything but I failed. My soul was suffocating.I wanted a happy life and to get rid of all. Sometimes my mind wanted freedom but my brain stopped me from that. Your Dadan never betrayed me, he loved me . Only loving always does not work in daily life. Money is another important source of happiness and we can't disagree with it. I have peace in mind that my Ashish became a good person. I am proud of him. That time I always prayed to God for him. I know my son makes the right decision so I give importance to his decision. So you also have to earn your mom's faith that you make everything right then she will not interfere in your life. The truth is parents don't want any wrong in their children's life. Did you understand my darling ". Susmita said.

" Great advice Granny ! Thank you. But I don't know when I will get my mom's faith. Or ever I will have it. Listen Granny , you are different. Dad always says ,' My mom is the best mom and best lady in my life. She never wanted anything from anyone. Whatever she did was all her own credit. Whole of her life she only served others. The first time she started writing and sending her stories to the Newspapers. I never appreciated her. Rather I deprived her by saying your stories will never be published. But she was determined. And one day they not only published her story but offered her to write for them. Your Granny is very optimistic. She always told me ,'Babu, everything would be fine.' So tell me if you are different or not? " Silpa replied.

Susmita said with a smile," I don't know how I am! But I think I am just a very common woman.Sometimes I think it was my luck that my married life was not normal. But in return God has compensated me after a certain time with lots of happiness like good friends, a good son and daughter in law and above all an excellent granddaughter."

Silpa became very happy. She hugged Susmita and said," I love you Granny."

In the meantime Ashish and Rina came back. Ashish told them the next morning they have to get up very early. They have to start for Gangotri at 4AM to 4.30 AM.They sat for dinner.

Rina said," Mom, I have talked to the hotel manager. They will take special care of you until we come. There may be some phone problems , but don't worry whenever we will get a chance we must contact you."

Susmita replied," Don't worry I will be fine. You all take care of yourselves."

Ashish said," Mom, what will you do alone these days? I am just thinking you can feel bored."

THE TOUCH OF BREEZE

THE TOUCH OF BREEZE(PART-13)

" Why should I get bored? During these days I will sit with my laptop and will add a few more words to my new novel and will try to finish it. You may not know why I agreed to come here. I have to write a love story. I didn't tell you. Around three and half months ago a publisher made a direct contact with me over the phone for my next novel. They requested me from the bottom of their heart and promised to pay me enough royalty. so I couldn't disagree." Susmita replied.

Ashish said," Mom, I am relieved to hear this." "That's why I was wondering why Granny agreed so easily to come with us! Granny! you are a chupa rustom'(Dark horse)." While saying Silpa laughed.

After dinner they packed the necessary things for Gongotri trekking. Then they went to bed early. The next morning they woke up soon. Ashish, Rina and Silpa started their journey to Gangotri after seeing off Susmita. She also sat with her laptop. Then it was 5 AM or 5 :30a.m

Last few days she didn't get time to write a single line. The publisher wanted a real and exclusive love story. So she started writing her untold love story, changing the name of the heroine. That time Ashish was in second year of engineering and went to a hostel. Then Susmita was about forty two. She never thought she would fall in love with someone at that age. But it happened and still she was bearing that love with her. There were adjustment problems with Arijit though they were living under the same roof.

She bought her first mobile phone. Ashish opened her Facebook account. She got lots of friends from there. One day she got a friend request from a young guy and accepted it. The guy was Sameer Dhuker. He was from Umbergaon,in Gujarat. Then he was twenty seven.

Susmita could remember the first day of their chatting. Sameer thanked her and told her about his family. He also said his name means wind or breeze .He had his parents, one elder sister and one younger brother. He was then trying for job. He also told her his nickname was Meva, which means sweet

Susmita also told him her name means lovely smile.In her personal life she loved to laugh loudly.Though very often it didn't happen. She also talked about her family. Ashish, Arijit and Nipa.She said she would call him Meva. And he was her little friend.

Sameer asked her in which name he would call her? She wrote," You call me 'mam', because I am used to hearing it for my students and the guardians".

Sameer replied," No I will call you 'Sus'. And you are my lady friend ". That was the beginning of their friendship on Facebook.

Everyday they chatted whenever they got time. It became a habit for both of them.If one day by chance they didn't text each other they missed it a lot.They started their day with 'good morning' and in the evening they shared their whole day with each other. He was vegetarian and Susmita was a Bengali with fish , rice so they chatted about food also. Six months passed in this way.

Once Susmita was very sad for Arijit's roughness and for some argument she didn't go to facebook for two days or text him. He became very worried and wrote," Hey, what happened to you? Are you okay? Please reply. You are not showing online. I need to talk to you. I missed you."

Then Susmita replied, " I am not well, I have some personal problems." He requested her continiously to tell him what was the matter! So she told him something about her married life. She thought Sameer was an unknown person so if she told him he would not gossip with her. She felt relaxed also. Always hiding in her mind that Arijit beat her or assault, made her suffocate.

The next day Sameer gave his phone number and told her to save it. At that time Susmita didn't know more about phones. Ashish did everything for her. So Sameer taught her how to save a number.

He said," Sus ,I was very worried about you. So please save my phone number. Then we can communicate very easily from WhatsApp. Don't worry I am with you. I am sorry for your life.If you feel sad or lonely please share with me. It will ease your pain ."

She saved his number in his nick name Meva .Then they chatted on WhatsApp. One year passed in this way. One day Sameer got a job and he gave her the news. Susmita became very happy. She invited him to come to Kolkata. While chatting with Sameer, Susmita told him that she had some relatives who live in Vadodara and Jamnagar. Hearing this Sameer wrote, "Sus, if you ever come to your relatives just inform me I will go to visit you."

While chatting with him she forgot about her real life. Sameer brought a fresh breeze in her life. That touch of breeze made her happy in that way that she always stayed with a smiling face. Arijit's rude attitude also didn't touch her. She literally stopped arguing with Arijit. She felt like she was not alone. There was someone who was far but always ready to stand beside her. What she didn't ever hear from Arijit after marriage. Time was going on.Ashish came from hostel very rarely. He said his study gets affected if he comes home. So after finishing tuition in the evening she and Sameer chatted before she went to the kitchen to make dinner. Arijit also remained busy with newspapers or Facebook. So he didn't take any interest in Susmita. Nipa watched Bengali cereal on T.V.Their chatting ended within 10 to 10.30 PM. Because Susmita couldn't wake up late at night as she was an early riser.

It was one Sunday. Arijit was not at home. Sameer wrote to her," Hey Sus, where are you? I want to see you. Can you send a selfie of yours?" Before that they only saw their pictures from Facebook. Susmita was not so interested in the phone. She only used it to call someone or chat with Sameer. So she didn't know how to take a selfie? Sameer wrote her all the instructions and Susmita read all and she learnt to take selfies and for the first time she took a selfie and sent him. Seeing her photo Sameer wrote," Sus I am speechless to see you. You are so beautiful,so cute .You look like thirty. I just can't imagine my lady friend is just like a young lady." She only replied," Ok".

Actually Susmita was feeling very shy. So she stopped chatting and showed him some cause of some work.Then she looked at the mirror and tried to understand, was Sameer telling the truth? Or lied? She thought as she was dark she didn't look beautiful. After marriage Arijit told her that," You may be dark but your face is beautiful with sharp eyes". Sameer's appreciation touched her heart. She discovered herself beautiful for the first time. Lots of time while fighting with Arijit she thought to finish herself. So many times she prayed to God for her death. As if she was living only to fulfill her duty to Ashish. But that was the first time she wanted to live. She never took any interest in her dress or make up. Then she thought if she did some make up then how it would be?

While she was thinking, another message came to her phone," Sus, believe me if I live near you I will certainly propose to you!"

Susmita wrote," Bap , insane ! Do you know what you are saying? I am your mam so do respect me. You are my little friend. So stay like that. Understood Meva?"

Sameer and Susmita's birthdays were on the same date but in different months. Sameer had 8th April and Susmita had 8th October. It was Sameer's birthday so Susmita greeted him on 8th April at 12 o'clock at night As she did to Ashish or Arijit. Sameer was so happy. He wrote," This is the first time in my life I got such an early wish. This is the best wish I ever had." Days were passing by quickly . Almost one year has passed since their friendship. Two different aged people without seeing each other face to face continued their friendship only by chatting. They were far but their attachment was so close.

Ashish got more busy with his studies.He had a goal to do a great result. Arijit stayed at home the whole of the day. He stopped his business after a heavy loss. Susmita worked hard from morning to night .The only refreshment in her life was Sameer. She waited for his text. She was like a drug addict about Sameer .Without chatting with him she felt sad. She read those chats again and again. Whenever she felt sad she only remembered Meva's name and photo of his face and it gave her an unexpected happiness. She was obsessed with him.

One day Sameer told her," Sus, listen open your Instagram account.I will share you my ID then we will follow each other and also can chat there." Susmita didn't know anything about it. So when Ashish came home on a vacation she requested him to open her Instagram account. They started following each other.

One day Sameer sent his selfie. And asked,"Don't feel shy tell me how I look? Do you like me? Am I looking hot?" Though from Instagram Facebook she saw his photos. But in the selfie he was looking very handsome, tall and fair. He has a massive beard. Though he was 28 he looked very mature. He had a silver band on his hairy left wrist which gave him a hero look. He wore a pink T-shirt. He had thick hair on his head with a nice haircut. Susmita replied," Everyone will like you. You are so good looking. Meva ,can I ask you something?"

" I didn't want to know if everyone would like me or not? I only want to know if you like me or not! Sure, ask me what you want to know? I have already told you about my family, my job." Sameer replied.

Susmita wrote," Uff baba, it's okay . If I liked you or not, that doesn't matter in your life. I like you as my little friend. I told you lots of time. I think my son Babu has a girlfriend. Don't you have a girlfriend?"

" Sus, don't say it like this. Your liking is very important to me. Yes I had a girlfriend, her name was Pretty Bhanushali. She was also Gujarati. You know some relationships can't work. So we got apart. Now I like someone very much and I don't know how to approach it. She doesn't understand me.Ok leave it,you see! We haven't seen each other directly. We don't know each other properly. Even though we stay too far away, our friendship is just wonderful. I don't know about your feelings to me but when I get your text my face glows with a smile. My heart beats more. And I can't express my happiness in words when I chat with you. I read our chat in the office so many times.When I share my day with you I feel relaxed. Tell me about your feelings honestly? Don't lie please. Your hobby is reading story books, right, you told me! Except for that, do you like something?" He replied.

Susmita didn't know what to say. She had the same feelings. She became like a teenager while chatting with him.She felt ashamed to say the truth.

She wrote," Meva ,I also feel happy. I love to chat with you. Because I don't get time to share myself with anyone except you after finishing my work. My husband doesn't want to hear as he is very busy with his work. Ashish is in a hostel. And mom loves to see TV cereal. So I spend my off time with my little friend. Nothing else. Hum my hobby is reading. I love to listen to songs. From my childhood I wanted to be a singer. Now if I feel any song is touchy I just practice it and sing it in the bathroom. That means I am a bathroom singer" Susmita replied.

" I also love songs. Can I hear a song from you! If you don't mind. Then record it on my WhatsApp, please". Sameer wrote.

CHAPTER FOURTEEN

THE TOUCH OF BREEZE

THE TOUCH OF BREEZE(PART-14)

So Susmita listened to a song of Asha Bhonsle, again and again from youtube and wrote it in her diary.

Arijit was a little surprised to see her strange behavior. He asked," Ei,what are you doing? Why are you listening to the same song too many times? It is very awkward." Susmita managed the situation somehow.

The next morning when Arijit and Nipa were sleeping, Susmita went to the bathroom and sang and recorded the first stanza of the song on WhatsApp. She was tensed if Nipa could wake up! Excitement was working to do this kind of thing. She heard her voice and realized that except for the wrong pronunciation of Hindi she sang well. Hindi(Indian national language and mother tongue of Sameer)! They chatted in English.Susmita said she would teach Bengali(Mother tongue of Susmita) in return he would teach her Hindi.It was a great feeling for Susmita.

When she joined her school then it was a party of teachers where new teachers had to do some performance. All thought except teaching an English Susmita didn't know anything. Headmistress said," Listen Susmita, if you can't perform anything then sing the school prayer song." But she surprised everyone by singing a very popular Bengali song. All clapped. Susmita always had passion for the songs. So after a long time singing for Meva gave her the same amazed feelings as that function's day. She was waiting eagerly to hear Sameer's reaction to her song.

Sameer praised her voice a lot. He wanted to call her over the phone to congratulate her. But she wrote ," Meva, please don't call me. I don't speak in English or Hindi at home. We only speak in Bengali. But you don't understand Bengali. So if I talk to you in English my husband can be curious."

Sameer wrote," I will call you for one minute. You only say 'hello Meva'.I want to hear your husky voice. Believe me, since I listened to your voice I fell in love with it."

Susmita stopped him at that time. She also wanted to hear Sameer's voice. Their chatting was going on about various issues. Maybe about politics or sometimes about Sameer's work or Susmita's work.

Then Susmita's summer holiday was going on. It was too hot at noon. Susmia installed an A.c at her bedroom. Because Arijit couldn't tolerate the heat. A.c was flying in Susmita's bedroom. Arijit was sleeping deeply. That time they had no physical relation in between them. Susmita didn't feel good. The whole day Arijit only tried to show him sick. He wanted more concentration from Nipa and Susmita. That felt Susmita intolerable. She was reading the newspaper lying on the bed. It was her long term habits. She always loved to keep herself up to date. Sameer's office was closed for some reason. Susmita got a message from him," Hey Sus, are you free? Can we chat sometimes?" I am feeling bored." Chatting to Sameer always made her happy. He never said anything fake to make her happy. They both told the truth to each other. But in between chats he always praised her and that gave her great pleasure.They started their chatting. After some time

Susmita wrote," Meva, if I have a daughter then I will think of you as my son in law. You are single now. You are handsome, tall and have a good job. Only one problem is that you are vegetarian."

" Sus, I am shocked to read you. Listen, you don't need to find anyone for me. I have already got someone. She doesn't understand my feelings. I don't want to give up. I believe one day she will love me madly". Sameer replied.

" Oh! That's it. You did not tell me.Is she from your office? How is she? Beautiful and fair like you! Congratulations Meva." Susmita replied.

Sameer wrote, " No, she is not from my office. She is from a different city. She is older than me. We met from an app. No, she is not fair like me. She is dark, short, and married. Yet I love her very much. Still I wasn't able to say her that.I don't know how to say her. But I am sure she also loves me very much. That she hides from me. Or she may be afraid to express it. I will stay beside her.If I have to go against the system of the society for that reason I will go. I am just waiting for her to understand that we love each other."

" Hum, then it is a big problem. Why don't you tell her directly that you love her? Then it will get solved. I am confused why do you love a married woman? You said your dad is very orthodox. You people marry in your community. Then why are you doing all this?" Susmita replied.

" I feel afraid to speak to her directly. If I hurt her. And for that reason if she stops all relations with me then! She is intelligent, educated and sensitive. So I am trying to make her understand. You will not understand Sus! Actually you have an arranged marriage.You never loved anyone. Her vibes match with me.I don't know how my time goes with her. If I don't talk to her I feel pain. I really don't know what is waiting for my future. But now she is my future.I hope one day she will understand me." Sameer wrote.

That time Arijit woke up and told Susmita to make tea for him. Susmita quickly stopped chatting, keeping her phone she went to the kitchen.She made Aloo paratha for evening tiffin and tea for everyone. When she again opened her phone she got the message," Sus, where are you? Are you busy? I have something to say to you." Susmita wrote," Talk to you later." That day they didn't chat anymore.

Next two days Susmita was very busy with a ritual that is called Jamai Sasthi!(Where a mom in law blesses her son in law with delicious food and gifts at her home.) Arijit didn't want to go to Susmita's house. Few years after marriage Arijit joined Jamai Sasthi.

Susmita had to take him forcefully. Then she gave up to request him. She went there alone, otherwise her mom would be sorry. She lied to her parents that Arijit was busy with work. And she wanted to meet her two cousin sisters who came with their husbands. That day her parents and uncle's family enjoyed a meal together. She took two costly sarees(For mom and aunt) , mangoes, sweets with her and went to her parents house that day. Going alone there she felt very sad.

Nipa also did Sasthi for the long life of her son. Her son in law was in Delhi. So she did not get a chance to do 'Jamai sasthi' but she did Sasthi. She gave Sasthi water to Arijit, Ashish and Susmita's head and blessed them with some new clothes.(Nipa took bath with a fan made from palm leaves under her navel with the name of Goddess Sasthi.The goddess of children.There were some ingredients like sixty grasses, paddy, sixty young shoots of bamboo and five types of fruits with stalks on the fan). The water on the fan she poured on their heads with paddy and grasses for their well. Susmita learnt the ritual from Nipa. She also did it for the good of Ashish.

After two days, Susmita wrote everything about Jamaisanthi to Sameer. Sameer wrote,"Wow! What a unique ritual! Sus, if I marry a Bengali lady then will my mom in law celebrate this ritual? By the way I missed you a lot.I know you were busy. "

" Hum! of course! Why not? If they have the ritual then they must will! But are you sure you are going to marry a Bengali lady? I mean why? You told me you have got someone. Is she Bengali? Is she from Kolkata!" Susmita wrote.

Sameer replied," Hum! She is from Kolkata. She has a husband. You didn't answer? Did you miss me or not?"

" Isss! What are you saying? She has a husband? Meva are you mad! How could you fall in her love? No , I didn't miss you because I was busy spending time with my cousin's sisters." Susmita wrote.

" Oh ! Didn't miss me! Yes I am her mad lover! Okay bye. I have some work. Listen, I have a project going on. So I would not be able to chat with you. You don't text me. When I feel free I will text you."

Saying that he became offline.

Three or four days passed. Susmita checked WhatsApp and Instagram to see Sameer online. She felt very lonely. Nothing was making her happy. Couldn't bear it she texted him,"Meva are you well?" Then she thought maybe Sameer could mind something so she deleted the message for everyone. Every night she got off her phone net so that her sleep didn't get disturbed anyhow. In the morning, keeping her net on, she saw Sameer's message,"What did you delete? Write it again. Don't feel lonely .I will chat with you after 8 PM. Have a great day."

Reading it Susmita's heart filled with happiness.Everything was looking beautiful. She looked in the mirror and saw her face was glowing.She felt that she could jump. She was looking so fresh. She thought of wearing a beautiful sari for school. After going to school one of her friends Pamela asked her," Susmita, what happened! Today you are looking awesome.Is there anything special or Arijit made love with you in the morning?" All smiled mischievously in the teachers room.

Susmita said shyly," Hey ! nothing, uff! You people are just incredible.I have nothing to say to you. Only I can tell that if you want to be a detective instead of a teacher you would be famous." All laughed loudly. Mitali said," Ei don't tease Susmita. Generally Susmita doesn't look at her dress up. But today's weather is good. So she wanted to wear a good sari. Is that right na Susmita?" Mistun said," Hey, Susmita di, really you are looking beautiful today. I always tell you to come to school with make up. You don't ever listen to me."

" You think whatever you can, I have my class now so I am going ." Saying that Susmita left for class.

After coming back home she finished her private tuition. She was waiting for Sameer's text but he didn't respond. It was 10 PM. She didn't feel good about having dinner.Her mind was feeling bitter. She quickly turned off the net connection on her phone and lay on the bed with a story book.

The next morning, opening her phone, she got the message from Sameer," Sorry please don't mind. Yesterday I was very busy with work. I worked till 11 p.m. I knew that you waited for my text .When I got free you fell asleep. I know that so I didn't text you."

Susmita felt angry with him. She thought she would not chat with Sameer anymore. She tried to make her mind in that way. Now she regretted that if that day she stuck with her decision then she would not have to suffer so much pain of loving someone madly.

After three days Sameer texted her on Instagram. " Sus how are you? I missed you a lot. My head was full of work and my mind was with you. With this confusion finishing a project was how tough you will not understand. My job is not so peaceful like you. Please reply when you will be alone."

Susmita thought not to reply. But she was defeated by her heart. At noon when Arijit was in deep sleep. She felt very lonely. She realized chatting with Sameer erased her loneliness. Especially that line from Sameer ,' My mind was with you', touched her heart. So she replied," I am well. No, I didn't mind."

Sameer was just waiting for the answer. He wrote immediately, " Oh! Very well. What are you doing right now? Are you alone and free? Do you have time for me?"

" Yes I am free. I am reading the newspaper. What are you doing?" Susmita wrote.

" I wanna chat with you seeing your beautiful face. I wanna hear you. I thought you would say , 'you missed me'. Sus, why are you so afraid of? Why do you hide everything? See, our life is valuable so enjoy it. Don't think too much. You know the over-thinkers spend their lives only thinking. Well I gave you lots of free knowledge. Though it is your right. As you are a teacher. Right!" Sameer wrote all with a smiling face emoji.

Susmita laughed when she saw the emoji. Her mind slowly filled with unknown happiness. She wrote," No no you are right. Sometimes a teacher also needs some knowledge, otherwise how could a teacher understand that she got a wise little friend in life in the name of Meva. Tell me all Gujaratiss are so wise? I heard

Dhirubhai Ambani was also a Gujrati. Ha ha ha ".

" Don't laugh! Think again what I said. We don't eat rice like Bengali and don't do politics like them! We eat chapati and do business! You know my dad always wants me to join his promoter business but I don't feel good. My brother Dixit will look at it.I like to live as I desire. So my opinion doesn't match with dad. During the holidays I have to sit at my dad's office." Sameer replied.

" Wow! This is very good. Actually you are a boy so you can do whatever you want. A girl can't do anything.We have to think ten times before doing something against the society. Meva, listen, evening is coming so I have to stop now. I have to lit a candle in front of God. So bye bye. Talk to you later. " Susmita wrote.

CHAPTER FIFTEEN

THE TOUCH OF BREEZE

THE TOUCH OF BREEZE (PART-15)

" Sus! Please wait for sometime! I have something important to tell you about my lover. I understood she hides everything. And she is very timid. Can you suggest to me how I can remove fear from her. Actually you are Bengali and she is also the same." Sameer wrote.

" Hey, how can I know? If you want my advice I can tell you that you are doing wrong. What will you get running after her? Don't take so much risk, go and like someone from your community and have a good life. Meva, listen, my mom in law is calling. Okay bye." Saying Susmita got offline.

Nipa was calling her. She went and lit a candle then got busy with evening snacks.

The next day Sameer wrote her ,"Sus! I am very upset about your advice. I thought you were brave. You must encourage me! As you are my lady friend. I was wrong.You are just like her.The truth is I love her. I don't know why?"

Susmita replied," Okay! I am sorry. It's your life. You do whatever you want to do.If you love her truly then go and tell her".

" Really Sus! Shall I tell her? She will not get angry with me na! Will she understand my

feelings?" He replied.

" See Meva, I think she will understand you. I don't know about her nature but as a woman I can tell you women can't be so cruel. Of course there are exceptions also. I don't think your love is so cruel.As she is older than you then I guess she is more mature than you." She replied.

He wrote," Sus! You know she is a very well behaved lady. She has lots of patience. I sometimes become surprised to hear about her daily routine. She is very hardworking and responsible . And I want her in my life. I can understand she is not so mature. She is very emotional. Shall I propose to her? Are you ready, Sus?"

" What does it mean, are you ready Sus! Hey ! Go and tell her, Meva. Not me! Crazy one! Susmita wrote with surprise.

Sameer wrote, " Sus! I only wanted to practice. She is also a teacher like you. So I wanted to see the reaction. Nothing else!"

" Meva! What are you saying? Is it a drama? That you need to rehearse. Go and talk to her directly. Whatever is in your mind. Ok I am going to stop. Today is Sunday. So I think she is also free. Don't waste time." Susmita wrote.

Sameer replied," Sus! Sus please wait. Why are you in such a hurry? I am telling directly to her. Listen please. Susmita I love you. You are that lady. I know it's very uncommon. But our heart doesn't follow any rule.I couldn't stop myself thinking about you. All the time you are coming to my mind. The whole day I imagine you. If you ask me what is the future of our love? I don't have any answer. But without you I can't imagine anyone in my life. Sus,I know what I am saying is unbelievable. A young guy falls in love with an aged woman. But it is very true. Sus, please accept my love my Jaan. If I live in Kolkata I will propose to you with a kneel down in front of you. Though I dream so. Sus, please try to understand my heart."

" Meva! Are you insane? I am a married Bengali woman. See my age. I have a son just a few years younger than you. You are telling me that I am that lady! No, no this is totally wrong. What do you want? Don't you understand how crazy you are! You are joking! Now I got you.' Susmita replied.

Sameer wrote,"Sus! I am damn serious! Last two years we have been chatting. If you don't feel good then why do you like to spend time with me? I don't know what to do? I don't mind your age. You are important to me.I am madly in love with you. No one looks so beautiful like you. I don't want to harm your family life. I can't deny you. With you I find comfort in my soul. Tell me truly don't you feel the same? Please Sus my babe you are my whole world now."

" I like to spend time with you. That doesn't mean I can do anything. Ok now I am going. Let's talk to you later. I love Arijit." Susmita said.

" And also you love me! I know that. But you are afraid to tell it. You are trying to control your heart. Sus! Please don't do this my love. Listen babe, love is precious. We should respect it. We are far so no one will get any wrong within it. I am not telling you to leave your family. Or ignore your husband. Please favor me as your boyfriend. Ok bye take care Jaan."Sameer replied.

Next few days Susmita tried hard to ignore him. She kept herself more busy so that Sameer won't come to her mind. In the early morning she saw his face from a profile picture on Whatsapp. Then she didn't show her online. She felt as if she had become like a teenager forgetting about her age.Thinking to stop chatting with him forever made her empty. During this time she didn't argue with Arijit. When he got a hot temper she just thought about Sameer.That there was someone far from her but loved her very much. After chatting with Sameer for so many days she began to love herself and her attitude changed about men. Her conscience said she was doing wrong but her heart said to stay happy. Love is crazy. It doesn't happen by judging anything. For Susmita,Sameer was a source of happiness in her dull life. Without chatting with Sameer she was feeling suffocated. Only Sameer could bring her smile back. So her brain was defeated by her heart. She also fell in love with Saneer. So after a week she texted him.

" Meva , I also don't know what to do but the truth is I also miss you so much when I don't chat with you. I don't know is it love or something. I think we should stop all for our good."

" No ,no, please don't say this. Did you miss me! I only want to know it. You missed me, that means you also love me. My babe, my sweetheart. Tell me once ,'I love you Meva'. Don't think about the future .Only live in the present. Make yourself happy. Then you will make everyone happy." Sameer wrote.

Susmita blew up with Sameer cyclone. She couldn't keep her strong. She tried hard to stop herself but failed. Sameer forced her to say to him ,' I love you Meva '.

She said," I love you Meva. I feel afraid that if my husband knows anything then what will happen! He is very ill tempered. You are so far how can I believe in you".

Sameer said ,'' Thank you Sus! For accepting my love.You don't know how happy I am. Babe, don't be afraid. Nothing will happen. Listen we stay very far so one will get to know our secret love story. Babe, you have to keep faith in me without any doubt of my love. As I believe you. Sis! I will stay beside you forever. Today I promise you my Jaan." Susmita asked what is the meaning of Jaan? He replied Jaan means life.

She felt so shy like a young girl. All the feelings were special to her. Arijit never said to her, babe, love, Jaan etc. So those words were new to her. He never showed her that love. She got a fresh breeze in her life as Sameer. Their love story started in this way.

Chatting became a habit in their life. Beautiful sweet words from Sameer made her forget everything about her age, her surroundings, her boundaries. Whole of the day her heart was covered with a touch of breeze. First time she realized Loving was so beautiful.Especially secret love. Whole of the day she stayed very happy. Meva was her teenage love which she never did properly.

Sameer told her," Sus, I imagine if we live near I will give you a ride on my bike and show you all the beautiful places of Gujarat. You will hold me tightly from the back and your silky hair will blow in the air and come to my face".

" Oh really! Meva,What will I wear to sit on your bike ?You must be in jeans! In my school there is a saree must. But at home I wear everything. " Susmita replied.

" Sus! We both will wear blue Denim jeans and white full sleeve shirts.And on the empty road I will take high speed so that you can scream in joy. Just imagine how much fun it will be. You will hold me from back tightly and your right palm will be on my heart.

Thinking about it, I feel so good that I can't express that in words. All day I sink into my imagination with you. You don't know how much I dream about us? Sus! Do you imagine like me? Just try to think and you will feel great." Sameer wrote

Susmita remained very busy the whole of the day. She didn't have time till evening. Though Ashish came from the hostel very rarely. Arijit didn't care about anything except his illness. Sometimes she felt guilty that she may be cheating Arijit. Then she felt very sad. Then a sin worked in her mind . Arijit assaulted her lots of times but she never thought of another man in her life. From childhood she saw how her mom, granny took care of their family. Susmita also started to imagine hearing from Sameer. It was a great experience. Sometimes she blamed her luck by thinking, "Why was she born so earlier than Meva?" It made her eyes moist.

One Sunday afternoon Sameer wrote to her," Sus! Why do you get silent sometimes? My love if you feel any pain just share with me. Sus can I say something if you don't mind."

" Meva ,sometimes I think I am cheating both of you. Maybe I forced you to fall in love with me. Then I feel very bad.See you have a future. What is the ultimate result of our story? I am anxious thinking about it. Tell me what you wanted to say?" Susmita wrote.

Sameer answered," Oh! my Jaan. What wrong did you do! I am an adult man. You didn't force me. I forced you. And look, you perhaps married

but that doesn't mean you can't love anyone. And I told you babe don't think about the future. Live for the present. No one knows about tomorrow. We can't predict anything. Life is full of miracles. Don't blame yourself for anything. You are theist hun! So just think God had planned to send me in your life. It is not coincidental. I wanted to tell you if we can see each other face to face for a while."

Susmita always felt happy with Sameer's beautiful words. She felt peace by reading all the lines.Then she asked in surprise," How will we see each other! Meva, are you coming to Kolkata?"

" No, how can I come to Kolkata without telling you? I don't know anything there except my Sus. We can see each other by video call. Just right now. If you agree then I will call you on WhatsApp and you have to receive it." Sameer wrote.

Before that Susmita never did video calls. She talked over the phone. She also wanted to see Sameer. So she agreed. Sameer made her understand how to receive the call.

Susmita went to the kitchen and closed the door. Every evening she made snacks so no one understood it. They saw each other by video call for two or three minutes but didn't say anything. They both smiled. Sameer showed her love sign by folding two palms. Susmita didn't know how to do that sign.It made her laugh. As if they were just two kids.

CHAPTER SIXTEEN

THE TOUCH OF BREEZE

THE TOUCH OF BREEZE(PART-16)

Then Sameer wrote," Thank you love, for keeping my request. From today I am gonna love you more. Do you know Sus? How sweet your smile is! You look so simple. But so pretty. Nothing is fake in you. Now tell me how I am? And by the way why didn't you show me a love sign? Next time you have to show it. Now tell me how I look?'

Sameer was tall and handsome like in his photo. He wore a light coloured t-shirt. He looked very modern. His haircut was perfect with his face. He was so fair that his lips were looking pink. His face was full of beard and mustaches. When he laughed his full jaws opened out. He was looking very wise too.

Susmita's love story was going on. Ashish did an excellent score in semester. He was just the opposite to his dad. He was a very cool, calm , serious type of guy. When he came, Susmita made new recipes for him by watching YouTube. He loved to eat like his dad. Ashish had lots of faith in his mom.Susmita felt proud of him. When Ashish came home Arijit became more calm. Ashish loved his dad also. He understood his dad's pain. When he came home he sat with dad and played chase. Then Susmita had two precious things in life one was Ashish and another was Sameer.

Then Susmita and Sameer very often did video calls. It was almost two and half years. Sameer wanted to meet her. One day he said," Sus! My babe, I want to meet you. I will go to Kolkata. Tell me when can I come there?"

Susmita replied ," Meva, I don't go anywhere alone. Only I go to my parents house and school. I don't know the road of Kolkata very much ".

" You don't need to worry about it. I can roam your city with you. You just say when can we meet "? Sameer said.

Susmita replied," You can come during the Puja vacation. Then we get almost one month of holidays. That time our city Kolkata is decorated as a new one.There are lots of lights, pandals and all the places are gathered with people and with all Kolkata looks like the queen of city. But the problem is how can I meet you! This is not possible for me".

" Sus, by reading your lines I start to imagine I have met with you. I have caught your hands standing in front of everyone saying to you. I love you Susmita. I can't live without you. What will you do if we meet.Please say it. Don't be so realistic. " Sameer replied.

" Meva, you know if you come here I will take a bouquet for you. We will see Kolkata by a cab . Then we will eat in a restaurant. I know you are veg and I am nonveg. But both will sit together and that day to honor you I will also eat veg". Susmita replied

" Wow! Really! You know what I will do? First I have to find a big hotel. Then when you come I will kneel down and catch your hands and propose to you in front of all, ' Sus ,I love you'. Accept my love .You will come in a blue sari. You look beautiful with this color." Sameer answered.

That was a daydream for Susmita .They planned to do so many things without knowing the reality. For Susmita love was a friendship , a caring and a promise to not to hurt each other. But she and Arijit couldn't maintain those things.

She and Sameer both didn't know what they were doing? And why? In reality she was older than Sameer but he was more mature than her. Susmita was obsessed with Sameer. She was not able to move herself for Sameer's thoughts. Arijit didn't take care of anything. Everything had to be done by susmita alone. So she was tired. Getting Sameer in her life she felt relieved.

Once Sameer said to her," Sus, my darling, do you want to see your name on my chest? I will get a tattoo on your name. I want to prove my real love to you. You are all mine. I imagine you as my wife. I talk to you alone, I sleep with you. Tell me ,are you mine or not? Does your husband touch you?"

Susmita felt very anxious. She felt she would harm Sameer's life. She had to stop everything immediately. So she tried to make him understand

"Meva! What are you saying? Our love is not like that. We both know it. No, you don't need to get a tattoo. You will get hurt. I love you, this is true.I can't harm your life. I am going to be old. You need to get someone your age. I am not right for you. No, I don't let my husband touch me. I am yours . Don't dream about me. We love each other but there is no reality of our relationship. You know it. Going against nature is thrilling but there is no happiness in it . All the time loving does not mean to be adamant to get someone but sometimes it is a sweet memory which we take to us when we die.You are my that love. I will go from your life when you will get someone." Susmita said

" Why do you always say you are old? I told you, your age doesn't bother me. I got you. I don't need anyone. I want to stay good. You are perfect for me . I am yours only. I will not allow anyone to touch me except you.And for that if I need to wait for my whole life I agree. I believe one day you will be my wife.I wrote your name in my heart. You know Sus! In our marriage there is a ritual of Mehendi. Where the girl's name is written on the boy's hand and boy's name on the girl's hand. Today I wrote your name on my hand.I want to see my name on your hand." Saying that he sent a photo of his hand with her name.

Susmita started hating herself. Her conscience told her as a loose character. She told herself," Why am I doing everything! Only to stay happy? If I truly love him then he must be free. She realized her love game with a younger guy should be stopped. Otherwise the end of it will be dangerous.

So she wrote," Meva, Meva my little Meva .Please don't be angry. I know I love you blindly. I don't get peace and I feel guilty when I think your life will be spoiled for me.Meva I will always be yours. My love story is rare. It is not for a happy ending. You will not get anything if you wish me as your wife.I can't leave Arijit and my family. I am really getting older . So please get someone and help me relieve".

Sameer replied," Again same words. Fuck your someone.I told you lots of time don't say all. You don't listen to me. Ok from today we broke up. I am going to block you from Facebook, Instagram and WhatsApp. So we can't contact each other. You want me out of your life. Live your happy life with your husband". And he blocked her from everything.

Susmita thought she would slowly forget him. She felt peace thinking that. But already three years have gone by. It was not easy for her to forget everything. But she controlled herself. After ten or twelve days for some reason Arijit got very furious. After stop talking with Sameer, Susmita was very disturbed. So she argued with Arijit and he slapped Susmita. Susmita couldn't control herself; she also slapped him. Whole day she cried and didn't take food.At night Arijit slept early while taking sleeping pills. Susmita felt so lonely. She talked sometimes with Ashish over phone.Didn't tell him about fighting. Because he didn't like it at all. During that time Sameer taught her lots of things like SMS. Then she sent an SMS to Sameer's number. He was the only one with whom she felt happy to talk.So she wrote an SMS to his number ," How are you Meva? I tried not to disturb you but failed. I am very sad today. Will you please talk to me sometime? I need you as my good friend."

He unblocked her from Instagram and texted," What happened to you Sus? Are you well? I am sorry for that day. Please forgive me. I didn't keep myself calm. I knew you would not stay without me.I missed you a lot. Don't ever say ,' get someone ' and I don't want to be your friend. I want you as my girlfriend. I want you ,only you. Now tell me what happened ?"

Susmita told him about fighting with Arijit. But never told him about physical assault. Sameer said to her that he would always stand beside her.So she should be happy to think that she had a handsome young boyfriend. Also said,"Please Sus! Don't make any arguments. If he says something wrong just keep silent. I am yours and you are mine. Keep it in your mind then you will feel happy and you will not go to any kind of fighting. I feel worried about you."

This line,' you are mine I am yours always made her more attracted to Sameer. While typing on the laptop her eyes filled with water. So many years had passed but she didn't forget Sameer a little. She could memorize every chat. While some of Arijit's memories faded from her life. She still didn't understand why she behaved like this? What happened to her at that time? If she stopped everything when he blocked her then she didn't have to bear the pain of her secret love till then and not to cry for it.

Susmita was a serious teacher and very reasonable in her entire life. She never thought to betray Arijit.God knows why didn't she control her mind to Sameer. Once Susmita cut her one finger while chopping vegetables. In a video call Sameer saw this and he said," You have cut your finger. Why didn't you tell me? Have you used some medicines or not? Be careful Sus. When I will be with you. I will cook. You don't need to do everything alone. We will do everything together. You know I help my mom make dinner."

Sameer was so caring. These little things forced Susmita not to forget him. Arijit also saw that cut but he never bothered it. He always remained busy with himself. He was very concentrate oriented. Arijit always wanted everyone to love him because he was mentally sick.

Susmita is a theist. She believes in God very much. She had a faith that whatever happened in our life all are God's plan. That's why she took Arijit as her luck.Every early morning after bath she worships God. And pray to Him to keep everyone happy including Sameer.

Their love story was going well again with chatting and sending messages.On Sameer' s one birthday she sent him a certain amount of money to buy gifts for him. On the other hand, Sameer wanted to come to Kolkata eagerly. Susmita thought of telling him to come to Kolkata during Durgapuja time. Then she thought it would not be right. She was in a dilemma. She didn't want to lose Sameer or couldn't accept him totally. All the time fear and sins worked in her mind. She tried to stop contact with Sameer but it was painful.

In the meantime Arijit planned for a short tour of a hilly village for four days. Susmita didn't want to but Arijit requested her continuously so she agreed. The spot was Echhegaoun from North Bengal. After going there Susmita felt so relieved. All around were fog covering the deepest forest of Oak and Deodar trees. Light cold, narrow hilly road and greenery took her mind far away from Kolkata. She knew Arijit became a new person when he went for a trip. He then became a very romantic man. That's why she was always grateful to Arijit. That man introduced Susmita seeing the outside except of of her surroundings.

At night Arijit asked her," Hey, what happened to you? You have changed a lot.Are you in some affair? Why don't you let me touch you? Earlier we have quarreled lots of times but then everything became normal".

Susmita replied with a light smile," Do you think so? I don't go anywhere except my school. How can I meet my lover!"

" Hum that is also a matter. I don't know, maybe you bunk school and go to him. But no! I am sure you will not do it. You love your school very much. See , if you are really in someone's love then stop it. You are very simple and you believe in everyone! Otherwise at last you will get hurt badly. I know the pain. Hey , what happened! Why does your face look like that? Are you serious! Uff, I am joking. You haven't left me after so many fights so I am damn sure you will not deceive me at this age! Listen , here we will roam on foot and after two days we will move to Darjeeling."

CHAPTER SEVENTEEN

THE TOUCH OF BREEZE

THE TOUCH OF BREEZE(PART-17)

Arijit was saying continuously. She didn't listen to anything. Her heart was beating fast. 'You will not deceive me' this line was heating her like pin bolting. That night she couldn't stop Arijit from making wild love with her. They kissed and had awesome sex. After a long time Susmita was very satisfied with Arijit's extreme love. Then she kept her head on Arijit's broad chest and cried for some time. She thought to tell him the truth," I am cheating you". But she couldn't .

Arijit said to her," Hey! Why are you crying? Why are you doing that? I was kidding. What a fuck! I am sorry! I know you can't do any wrong! Ok let's sleep now. Tomorrow we have to wake up early! If we are lucky we can see the Kanchanjanga ." Saying all he fell asleep. Susmita thought after going back to Kolkata she would stop all relations with Sameer. She was tired from playing that game. They enjoyed the trip very well. They came back with a fresh mind. That was the last trip of susmita with Arijit.

Susmita didn't tell anything about the trip to Sameer. She only said she would be busy with a function.She was offline to avoid Sameer. When she went online she got lots of texts from Sameer," Hey Sus, my love! Where are you! Why are you not showing online? How busy were you? That you didn't get time to wish me good morning. You know my day goes well if I get wishes from you. Are you Okay Sus? You didn't get a fever or something na! I am worried.If you don't reply then I will call you. You know I am atheist. But this is the first time I prayed to God to give me a chance to meet my Sus!" The texts were coming one by one. Susmita was forced to reply,"Meva, don't worry .I am good. Don't you know that I have a family. I have to maintain some duties towards it. What do you want! Shall I get out of the house? I told you I would be busy with a family function."

" Okay, I understand Jaan, but I deserve a hello from you .Sus I don't want to hurt you. I love you madly. I don't want a single harm in your life. When I know that you are good I feel good. I want to see you. I want to go to Kolkata. Tell me the time please." Sameer wrote.

"Listen Meva, I think my husband has understood something about my affair with you. So don't text me at any time. I will text you when I feel safe. Now forget about Kolkata. And forget about me also. Let me handle it." Susmita replied.

Sameer wrote, "What! Did he doubt you? Or tell you something wrong? Please stay calm.Don't be tense.Everything will be fine. Sus! I will wait for your text".

" Meva , please don't do that. I beg you. Don't spoil my life as well as yours. What we are doing it's a kind of insanity. Our love story is good for reading but worse for real. It never happened in the world. I am married and have a young son.You are my teenage love let it stay as it is. This happy memory we will take with us at the end of us. When we will be aged we will memorize it sitting alone. All love stories are not for good endings. You will always remain in my heart. No one can see you. I will keep you a secret in my soul. But I can't do these wrong things anymore. This kills me.Think of me as a cheater. I have cheated both my husband and you. Please, I apologize for everything. You are a young and handsome man and you will get your soulmate easily. I am forty five now. I am much older than you. If you love me you will never have a family or happiness. Get someone please and have a great life. And make me free. Don't make me cry more please. Let me forget everything. I am not perfect for you.I don't know but if I have another birth then I will wait for you .This time I am only for my husband. If you come to Kolkata after marriage then come to my place." While Susmita was typing all her tears were rolling down. She was lying. She knew forgetting Sameer was not so easy. Only she wanted to make him free for his next life.

" Oh! That's it. I know you are lying. You love me . I am tired to hear your whine story. If you can live happily with your husband forgetting me then okay. No Susmita, you are not a cheater. You are a coward who has no guts. In fact you will never love anyone because you are very realistic. You always try to know the end. Love doesn't always mean to get married. It means an attraction, a feeling which makes us alive. You know who are happy in life? Those who let themselves flow with the time. I am happy with you without marrying or without giving any name of my love. Bye then. Stay happy forever." Sameer stopped chatting by writing it.

Then he wrote a big article on his Instagram account about his wishes and how to make them accomplish. Susmita understood he wrote everything on them. About one month they didn't have any connection. Though she wanted to know his news but stopped herself. Everyday she went to his Instagram account to check his new post.Seeing each other online was their only communication.

One day when she came from school Nipa told her," See Susmita, Ari is feeling chest pain from morning. He took some medicine but it didn't work".

She asked Arijit," Hey ,what happened? Let's go to the doctor. Don't worry, you will be fine." Arijit replied in pain," Ei, listen I can't tolerate pain anymore. It is unbearable. Do something now.". Susmita immediately took him to their family doctor.The doctor told her to admit him in the hospital fast as he guessed it was a heart attack. Susmita soon hired a cab and ran to the hospital. Whole of the way Arijit caught her hands tightly. Trying to say something. He was feeling savior pain. After reaching there she knew Arijit had passed away in the cab. Susmita was speechless. She never thought that could happen.While getting down from the cab she untied her hands from Arijit forcefully and ran to the doctor. She didn't understand that Arijit left her hands forever.Maybe he was trying to beg her mercy at last. Susmita gave her company at the last breath of Arijit. When she got the news of Arijit's death she couldn't hold her. She caught his feet and cried," Forgive me. I am responsible for everything. I couldn't keep my promise while marrying you. That's why it all happened. "

He didn't give her a chance for his treatment. All the family members were shocked to hear the news. Arijit was mentally sick but physically was very strong. Always concentration oriented Arijit at the end left without waiting for anyone's concentration.

Ashish came from the hostel. He didn't believe his dad's sudden death.

Nipa always said to Arijit,"Ari, don't take too much painkiller. At old age you have to suffer with kidney problems. And we all will suffer for you." When Arijit's dead body came from the hospital Nipa started crying by saying," Ari, you always wanted to live your life in your own way! .At the end you proved it my boy. At the time of death you didn't bother for anyone. As a mom I am a failure. God has given me the right punishment. Otherwise now is the time for my death. Instead of me He has taken you. How can I bear this pain? Forgive me, my son." She was crying.

Ashish hugged her and said," Amma , don't cry. We have nothing in our hands. I am here for you."

Getting the news her only sister in law came from Delhi. That time their house became a mourn house. All were crying. Ashish did his dad's last rituals. Their house became full with relatives and friends. Though Arijit did not like most of the relatives.

Susmita became a widow at the age of **45**. She never thought about it in her dream. That Arijit could leave her so early. Arijit took her married sign bangles and Sindoor with him from her life.

After everything their house became empty. All the relatives went back. Ashish and his only aunt Aritri stayed for a few days. Suddenly Susmita became duty less. Buying medicines for Arijit, giving them in time, making tea for him, making food for him all stopped within a moment. Susmita felt so empty. She didn't feel good at anything. Especially in their bedroom. When she entered there she had a feeling that Arijit was reading the newspaper. They had no physical relation but Arijit slept beside her. After his death Susmita felt scared on that bed alone. Her eyes filled with tears remembering Arijit. She thought herself as the worst. Arijit was not like normal people. He never took any responsibilities of family work that were valueless to him. He didn't do anything in life but never felt hesitant to tell the truth. He never put his head down in front of his mom or wife. He loved to see the world and know about different places was his passion. Most of the famous tourist spots of India he roamed with his small earnings. Without taking any responsibility how a man can lead a life Arijit showed. His sudden death changed Susmita a lot. A regret came to her mind. She said to God," I stopped loving him that's why you took him to you. forgive me Lord."

Ashish saw his mom as a strong lady. After his dad's death he saw his mom broke down. So he felt something to do. His mom had to look after the family and Amma Nipa. So he thought of connecting her with some creative work.So that she could be busy with it.

One day he told Susmita," Mom, you love writing and story reading. There is an international platform where people share lots of things. I am going to download it on your phone. In your off time you spend time there. You will not feel alone."

Susmita started writing there.It made her happy. Whole of world got to know her name as a story writer from that platform.After finishing all her work in the evening when Nipa saw TV cereals then she expressed her words. People praised a lot of her simple writing. Six months had passed. Susmita and Nipa were going to be normal.If sometimes Susmita cried for Arijit then Nipa said to her,"Don't cry Susmita, we can't control everything in the world. Ari never loved his life. He tried to kill him so many times. . So God has made him free from his dirty life. Everyday I pray to God to give him a happy and peaceful life in next birth." Though Nipa alone cried in front of Arijit's photo. Every early morning Susmita kept some white flowers in front of Arijit's photo. When Ashish came he made both of them understand to take everything normally. Life was going on.

One day on her Instagram account she showed her tribute to Arijit and wrote a poem on him and shared it with his photo ." When you were alive I didn't give you value. After leaving me you showed I never had that capability to value you. Stay happy where you are. Forgive me." That time Sameer blocked her from WhatsApp but not from Instagram. They had no connection in between them. After seeing the tribute he unblocked her from WhatsApp and messaged ," Hey , Susmita, what happened to your husband? I don't know anything about it. I am very sorry. Please answer me."

CHAPTER EIGHTEEN

THE TOUCH OF BREEZE

THE TOUCH OF BREEZE(PART-18)

That day was their marriage anniversary day. Arijit chose that day to make their marriage day memorable. The day was 22 Sravan, the death day of Rabindranath Tegore. Susmita was very sad from morning . She was working with tears and she understood she loved Arijit very much."

Susmita didn't reply. She thought not to keep any relation with Sameer. She deleted his phone number. Then he called over her phone continuously . So at last she received his phone and started crying ,"Listen Sameer, only for me Arijit died so early. I fell in love with you without understanding anything. I was cheating on him. God has given me the punishment to make me widow. All happened only for my insane love."

Sameer said," I know you are sad. But don't talk like nonsense. You are educated! Hun! Then how can you say this? You believe in God. Don't you! You always think God has planned everything in our life. So don't blame our love for this mess. Don't regret Sus! Don't say any wrong word about our love. We loved each other. There was nothing wrong in it. Time will heal everything. Take your time."

Time was flying. In the meantime Sameer texted Susmita to know about her. Susmita told him that she started writing. Sameer became very happy. Ashish wanted to study M tech in Delhi. At that time Ashish and Rina became friends. Rina also wanted to go there. Before going to Delhi Ashish stayed at home for four months.

Rina also came to their house very often. When Ashish remained at home their house was full of fun. Because his friends came and they enjoyed the party. After he went to Delhi their house became empty again. Susmita felt very lonely. Most of the time Nipa slept or watched T.V. After finishing her writing at night her loneliness killed her. Sameer's birthday was coming. She tried to stop her mind but failed. So one day she texted him," How are you Meva?

After two days he replied" I am okay. What about you? Are you still writing? I am happy that you remembered me." And thus again their chatting started.

Now Susmita started loving Sameer's company more because of her loneliness. One day Sameer called her over a video call and saw her. Then he told her," Sus you are looking so dull without Sindoor (A red powder which married women put on their hairline for the long life of their husbands). Why do you leave your earrings or bangles? Please love yourself. See, our life is a surprising mixture of sorrow and happiness."

The beautiful words of Sameer always touched the heart of Susmita. He was fifteen years younger than her but his words were very right. She wrote, " I am a widow, Meva. I don't have the right to use Sindoor. You know my mom in law became a vegetarian after losing her husband. Within one year of someone's death in the family we don't do any holy occasion at our home. Bengali widows have to maintain so many rituals. Ashish didn't let me become a veg or do so many rituals ."Susmita replied.

Sameer replied," Exactly , see who has gone, they never will come back but who are alive they are important. I agree with your son.I know you are a widow. You are a woman first. Don't think of yourself alone please. I am always with you. Sus! Now you are free! If you want and if you love me then we can get married." Sameer said.

" What! Are you mad or something! How will we get married? Hun! You may have that courage to come to Kolkata to marry me but I don't have that strength .Then how can we get married! By online? You made me laugh a lot, Meva"? Susmita said.

," yes you are right. We will get married online. Like our online love. When your husband's one year death anniversary will pass then we will do it. I will put Sindoor on your hairline and then we will pronounce that Mantras. We will become husband and wife. I will go to you at the right time. Now we will be engaged. Sus! My love! Please don't oppose it. It will make us happy. Please do agree. We both understood that we feel happy with each other's company. So let's do it. It will improve our relationship." Sameer wrote.

Susmita couldn't think more. She said ," Meva, people will call us mad. What are we doing? I don't know what you will get by this? Are we crazy?"

" Yes , we are exceptional. Let us live in that way. Who wants to laugh? Can laugh. You don't worry about me. I feel happy with you.Listen, you don't think too much. Because all the time your over thinking spoils everything. One day our love story will be famous. We are the inventor of online marriage. He wrote it with a smile emoji.Today I am very happy, Sus, to spend time with so long. I missed you.Tell me didn't you miss me? Don't lie. God's promise." Sameer asked.

"Yes, I missed you Meva. Now I am scared of the future ." Susmita replied.

" Nothing will happen.I told you not to worry too much. Let's flow with the time. I love you ,Sus! You love me . And that is the truth. My babe." Sameer wrote.

So after Arijit's one year anniversary they decided to get married. Susmita had no option. She couldn't deny Sameer's love from her life trying thousands of times.What was that! love or obsession Susmita never found out the answer in her whole life. She only knew Sameer was her that love which she never would explain to anyone. Other people could call her crazy or lose character but for her he was just an unforgettable love.

That day one of the brothers of Nipa took her to his home for an occasion. Ashish was in Delhi.Susmita was alone at home. As planned in the evening Sameer called her on video call. Susmita wore a beautiful saree. Sameer took Sindoor at his finger and put it on the phone screen where Susmita kept her head. Then they both pronounced the mantras " I am yours you are mine".

Sameer looked so happy. He said,"Sus, put the Sindoor and look at you in the mirror! You are looking so beautiful. I can't imagine that from today you are my wife. Please, Sus! Promise me you will put on the sindoor everyday on my name. I want to get you as my wife." Then Sameer kissed on the phone screen and told her to do the same. Susmita obeyed him. Then he asked," Sus ,are you happy? From today you are not Susmita Sen. You are Susmita Dhuker. I am feeling horny by thinking about this."

Susmita replied," Yes I am feeling so delighted. Yes, from today I am Susmita Sameer Dhuker. Let me touch your feet. You know the Bengali wife takes blessings from her husband. You are my Bor. Bor means blessings. I promise I will put Sindoor in your name till my death.

He said," Sus! My Jaan, don't be afraid. Keep in mind your Meva is always beside you."

That day Susmita behaved really weird. She didn't know what happened to her? The feeling of getting married to Sameer in that way was very special. She didn't know the real cause of her happiness. They wanted to talk more. Nipa came back. So they stopped. That time Nipa and Susmita both slept on Susmita's bed. So they couldn't talk at night.

After typing these Susmita heard a knock at the door. She opened the door and saw the hotel service boy.

He said," Mam! Your breakfast is ready. Shall I serve here or will you come to dianning hall?"

Susmita didn't realize it was already 9 AM.She sank with writing. She said," No, No I am coming into the dining hall. Thank you."

She went to the washroom. After changing her night dress she wore a saree and went to the hall. Her knees were in pain. Sitting on the laptop for a long time. She saw lots of people were having breakfast. She sat at an empty table. They served her mixed veg paratha, curd, pickle and sweets. She was just going to take a bite. A young man about thirty years old told her," Mam, can I sit here?

Actually all the tables are full of people!"

"Yeah, no problem, please be seated." Susmita replied." Thank you Mam, I am Rupankar". Saying it he sat down.

They both started eating. He asked," May I ask you something mam! Are you Bengali? Your talking style shows that. Maybe I am wrong. I stayed in Kolkata for two years for my job."

" Oh! That's it. You are right. I am a Bengali! I am Susmita Sen. So where did you live in Kolkata? And where is your origin!" Susmita asked.

" My origin is in Odisha. We live in Bhubaneswar, the capital of Odisha. My mom is a Bengali Muslim and Dad Odia.My maternal uncle lives in Park circus. Though I never went there. I heard it all from my mom. My grandpa disowned my mom for getting married to my dad. I wanted to meet him but didn't give me his address. " Rupankar replied.

They were talking while having breakfast. Susmita was feeling good. She understood that the guy was very free. Susmita asked him," Oh! That means In Kolkata you lived near to me.Me from Jadavpur, very near to Ballygunge. So what do you do by profession? When did you come here?"

" Mam, you live in Jadavpur. One of my friend's houses is near Jadavpur University. I went there many times. I am a bank employee. State Bank. I came here with my parents yesterday. My parents will go to Gangotri temple while fasting so they didn't eat breakfast. I would not feel good by eating alone. My pleasure I met you. Are you alone? I can't see anyone with you?" Rupankar said.

" I came here with my son, daughter in law and only granddaughter. Early this morning they went to Gomukh. So I am alone." Susmita replied.

" Wow! Good. I will start tomorrow. My parents will stay at the hotel. He answered. After breakfast when they had tea Susmita saw a very beautiful ,fair lady was coming towards them with a gorgeous saree. There was a dark, tall, fatty , little aged man with a bald head coming after her. The woman had Sindoor on head and bangles in hands. Coming near to the table the lady told Rupankar," Baban, seeing your late we have come here. We are not supposed to be late for the temple?"

He replied" No, mom, don't worry. We will go in time.Mom, see she is near your parents house." And then he turned to Susmita and said," Mam, meet my parents." Susmita folded her hands and said to them," Nameste". They also did the same.

The lady asked," We will talk to you later. Do you like to take a walk to the temple with us?" Susmita replied," No thanks, you go. You will enjoy it a lot. I have done all with my son. I am staying at room no: 203. Please come in the evening for a chat. I will be very happy."

Rupankar said," Thank you mam, yes we certainly will. Ok bye now". They went away. Susmita returned back to her room.

In the meantime Silpa called her. She was shouting with excitement," Granny ,are you okay? We are well. You know we are still walking and walking. What a beautiful place! I can't say you in words. Lots of people are walking with us. Listen now I am keeping. Stay well. I can't hear you properly."

Susmita again sat with her laptop. She started writing again. The next day she got a beautiful text for Sameer." Good morning my Susmita Dukher. My love. You know last night I only dreamed of your face .Now I am waiting when I really will see you directly. Sus! I want to see your face with Sindoor. Please send it to me. I want to see it before leaving for the office."

Susmita went to the bathroom and after putting Sindoor on head she sent the photo of her face. Then she cleaned everything. So that Nipa couldn't see it.Then again a bad thought came to her mind. If something happens to Sameer for not putting Sindoor on his name. So she quickly put Sindoor on the back side of her head and covered it with her hair. And promised that she would always put Sindoor on her Meva's name so that he could live long happily.

In the evening Sameer wanted to know, " Sus! How much do you love me? Are you happy? Or you are doing everything to keep my word."

" No, Meva, I am very happy. You know I am a widow. A Bengali widow never put sindoor. But I love you very much. So I can do everything for you. And I promise I will love you till the last day of my life."

THE TOUCH OF BREEZE

THE TOUCH OF BREEZE(PART-19)

While typing she fell asleep. As she woke up very early in the morning. When she woke up she saw it was 1PM. Then she quickly took a hot water bath. Then she came to the hall for lunch. They served her rice, ghee, brinjal fry, dal, one veg curry, paneer and curd. She looked around but didn't see Rupankar or his parents. When she came back to the room she got her brother's call. Her brother Sumit and his wife Payel loved her very much. She has only one niece working in Bengaluru. Her dad died so many years ago. Mom does not have that much problem but she has knee pain. But this is a peace for her that Payel takes good care of her mom. She talked with mom and Payel also.

There was a TV in the room. She loved to read the newspapers but after going there she didn't get any newspaper so she wanted to know the news update. She opened a Bengali news channel. The Durga puja of Kolkata has finished. Only the bamboo for the structure of the pandals was left here and there on the side of the road. The Bengali people had to wait for one year for the next puja. While she was watching the news she heard a knock at the door. After opening the door she saw Rupankar and his parents. She said to them," Please come on in. Have a seat!"

Rupankar said," Thank you mam. My dad and I are going to the reception for tomorrow's Gaumukh trekking. Mom wants to talk to you."

" Hey, please come. Saying that Susmita turned off the TV and gave her a chair. Both dad and son had gone. Susmita realized that the lady was very beautiful at her young age. She looked very smart.

Susmita asked," How was Gangotri Temple? How was your experience?" Oh sorry I didn't ask your name? I am Susmita. I know you are from Park Circus."

She replied," I am Firdous Mahanto. I think you are older than me so I will call you Didi(Elder sister). Gangotri temple is beautiful. And the views are just stunning. My son didn't want to come from there. We worshiped Goddess Gangotri . You heard I am from Kolkata. I left that city around thirty years ago. When I heard the name of Kolkata my soul was lost somewhere. My husband Shankar Mahanto showed me most of the beautiful places of India but didn't take me to Kolkata again. When my son told me you are from Kolkata I couldn't stop myself from talking to you."

" Oh! I can understand that you love Kolkata very much. Then what is the reason for not going to Kolkata?" Susmita asked.

Firdous said," Didi , when I passed in class twelve and got admission to first year then our college arranged an excursion for four days in Bhubaneswar and Puri.My dad Rahim Sakhe was an orthodox Muslim. Five Times Namaz in a day was a must for him. He had a big leather factory in Park circus. He was a very influential person there. My family was very conservative .My dad didn't want me to join that excursion. I requested him lots of times. So he agreed. He loved me so much. My dad had five brothers and three sisters. No one had a girl child. So I was very adorable to everyone. Especially for my dad. I was his princess. My marriage was fixed with a rich Muslim boy . I visited Bhubaneswar with my schoolmates and teachers. We had great fun the whole day. At night I started vomiting because of food poisoning. My teachers took me near a Government hospital near our hotel. There Shankar worked as a junior doctor. My teachers or my school mates were not allowed to stay with me. Shankar had a night shift in my ward. So he took very good care of me. I was so afraid I was crying. Whole of night I made him suffer for me. But he had lots of patience. Whole night he visited me again and again. He caught my hand and took me to the washroom whenever I wanted to vomit. He sat beside my head and caressed his hand lightly on my hair , face and said " Don't be afraid. I am with you. You are going to be perfect tomorrow." That was the first time a man touched me. I didn't know anyone there. That night I heard only one name, Shankar. That night he became my savior. I fell for him. The next day I was released from the hospital. Shankar gave me some medicine. My teacher didn't inform my dad because he would be worried and could get angry. Before leaving the hospital I gave my address and our landline number to Shankar. After one week he called over our land line number and luckily I received it. We talked. He said after my leaving he missed me a lot. As he also fell in love with me.I felt so happy. Our love story started in this way. Sometimes we talked to each other over the phone. One day my dad called my fiance and his family to our home to get together for the occasion of Eid. They talked about our marriage date. I became worried. If my dad arranges for my wedding. That time without Shankar nothing was important in my life. So I told everything to Shankar. And he told me he would come and wait in the Howrah station. I would go there then we would flee to Bhubaneswar.I caught his hand and fled with Shanka. My dad found out with the help of my friends and he came to Bhubaneswar and tried to take me with him. When I didn't agree he threatened that if we ever came to Kolkata he would kill us. Not only that he sent his people to take me forcefully.In fear my dad in law sent us to Kerels .One of his friend's nursing homes was there. Shankar joined there and after having my son Rupankar we came back to Bhubaneswar again. That is the reason Didi".

" Oh! That means you never met your parents. But I think you are very happy to get him?" susmita asked.

" No Didi, after that I didn't meet them.I talked to my mom secretly. When I first talked to her she cried a lot. She told me my dad broke a lot. He got hurt for me and promised that he would never like to see me alive again.For him I am dead. After that he got a stroke only for me. Now he is well. Very rarely I talk to my mom to know about them. My two brothers got married. My dad and mom are happy with them. They forgot me. But Didi, now sometimes I feel sad. Sometimes my heart wants to see my family and enjoy being with them which I miss a lot. I got Shankar, it is true.It is true he and his family love me very much. But there is some regret in my mind .Now I realize I did wrong by hurting my dad so badly. I was so selfish only thinking about myself."she said with moist eyes.

" Oh! I see! That is so sad. Yes Firdous, you are right. Sometimes we make some decisions without thinking about the ultimate result but then we feel pain for it. Please don't regret it now. You are lucky to have your love. Stay happy with your son and husband ". Susmita replied.

In the meantime Rupankar and his dad came. Then they talk for a few more times.

After they had gone, Susmita opened her laptop again. Susmita was thinking love sometimes becomes crazy like hers and Sameer's. Susmita started writing about her story. Her laptop was getting filled with her secret love.

The next day Sameer wrote,"Sus, my babe, how are you? Did I come to your dream last night? You know the whole night I felt you were beside me. I want to see you now with Sindoor. I am making a video call."

Nipa was sleeping then. After Arijit's death she got up late from bed. Susmita quickly put on Sindoor and received his call. After seeing her he said," Sus, I am feeling so horney. Now we are married. When will we have our sex? "

Susmita said," Meva, you are so far away from me. How did you do it all? I am feeling shy. "

" What are you saying? Without sex our relationship will not run long Sus. Now see me". Saying it he opened her t-shirt. Susmita saw his beautiful manly body. His fatless body with a broad chest with bushy hair. His waist was slim ,his belly was thin and hands were looking strong. Arijit also had the same broad hairy chest. But he had a large tummy. Susmita was hesitant to look at his strong muscles body directly. It was really exciting to her. She never thought that seeing someone in this way could make a person so horny. The whole day Arijit remained without a shirt. She never got such a strange feeling.It was very new to her.

Sameer said with a light smile ," Sus! What do I look like? Did you like my body as your husband? Would you allow me to touch you? I showed you my upper portion naked. Now you show me your upper portion please and make me happy."

Susmita said," No, Meva , please don't say. I can't. I feel ashamed. I didn't tell you to show me. You showed it by yourself ".

" Hey ,hey we are married now. Don't feel shy. I love your shyness. If I requested you earlier to kiss me ,you would say I am your teenage love. But now I am your husband.I put you sindoor. I realized you don't love me like I do. Maybe I forced you. You only loved your husband. Susmita are you playing with me? We have been together a long time, but you don't believe me. When your husband was alive then you were confused. Now you are free but your attitude hurts me. I feel that I have told you to do something against your wish. If you don't love me then stop everything please. "Sameer said with upset.

That time Nipa woke up so Susmita stopped talking to Sameer. She was sad because she did not want to make Sameer unhappy. What she would say to Sameer she didn't understand.

At last she decided if really Sameer is her husband then she should keep her word.

So the next morning Susmita showed her upper portion of her body.Her breast and her stretch marks on belly also showed up. Susmita told him," Meva , you know I am dark and I gave birth to Ashish so I have stretch marks on my belly. Do you like them?"

Sameer was so pleased, he said," My babe, you don't know how beautiful you are with your darkness.It makes me excited. I saw your dark nipples and I just want to touch them. I will kiss on your stretch marks. You are important to me. Everything is valueless."

The next morning Susmita got his messages ," Sus ,my jaan last night I slept with you. I imagined that I had touched your beautiful and big breasts and you know I musterbate and felt so satisfied.

Listen my darling we are far but if you want to feel the happiness of love then just imagine that we are sleeping together as husband and wife. I kissed your whole body. And we made love. Please imagine whenever you sleep alone." Before that Susmita didn't know what musterbate was?

In the evening when Nipa was busy with TV Susmita lay on the bed and imagined Sameer as her husband and sleeping together. And Sameer was right.After a long time she felt that satisfaction of physical relationships. She was amazed how imagination makes everything so real."

Susmita started thinking of Sameer as her real husband though she never met him. In her dream everyday she slept with Sameer. And felt that orgasm. Some day in the early morning they did video calls.

One day Sameer sent her photos of his penis and his chest where he wrote her name. Susmita was surprised to see and asked him ," Meva how did you do it ? How did you write my name there ? You didn't get hurt." Sameer answered," I was horny. I imagined you as my wife and my penis became large. Do you like it ? Do you want to touch it? It's all yours Sus my babe.Now you have to show me my name on your breasts. Tell me when I will do that!"

Susmita felt so ashamed. She couldn't understand what to do! She had to make her Meva happy to show her naked body. On the other hand her female entity stopped her from doing that. She was always afraid if Nipa could understand anything. Throughout those days her love was platonic. But then it turned into sex.So her conscience didn't give her the permission to show her naked body to Meva.

One day Sameer showed her his naked body. And asked her," Sus! See me! My love. Take me to you. I want to see you full naked. I want to see your beautiful pussy.

Tell me when I will be lucky to see it. Then we will do online sex. And it will be wild."

Susmita replied," Meva, you know I love you madly and I can do everything for you. But please don't make me naked. I never will do it. When you come to Kolkata then you will make me naked by yourself." Sameer said,"Yes I will certainly come but I want to see it now. Show me please. You always say no whatever I request ".

CHAPTER TWENTY

THE TOUCH OF BREEZE

THE TOUCH OF BREEZE(PART-20)

" No, I can't do this. I did everything that you said. But please don't request me to do this.I am sad today." Susmita replied.

" That means you don't love me! I showed you. I didn't hesitate to do it because you are my wife." Sameer said. Susmita cut the call.

That day was Arijit's birthday. Susmita was very disturbed. Nipa was crying from the morning. Susmita was sad because on his birthday he liked to celebrate outside. So they went to restaurants for dinner. When in the evening Sameer requested her again to show her naked body. She got very angry. She said," When I told you I am not comfortable with it then you have to understand it. If you love me truly. You will never request me. Meva you only want to make yourself satisfied with my body. Go and find someone who can show you everything whenever you want."

"I know today is your husband's birthday. That's why I was trying to make you happy. You said that line again. What do you think? I will not get anyone! Okay from today we don't have any relation." He blocked her from WhatsApp and Instagram by saying it. Susmita didn't block him because she had an undoubted faith in her Meva that he loved her madly.

They stopped chatting and Susmita was a little bit happy to think that she had gotten him rid of her life. Sometimes it hurt her that she would destroy his life. Though she felt very lonely and tears came so she made herself more busy with writing. She was very regretful about her wrong decision to show him her body.

Four months later one day suddenly she saw an Instagram post by a young lady for Sameer . She was a follower of Susmita's Instagram account. Her name was Jingky Duerte. She made a portrait of Sameer's profile photo and posted it on her account. She also wrote some romantic lines on Sameer. Seeing it Susmita became curious .She texted her," Hey, I am Susmita from India .Where are you from? Your painting is beautiful. Who is this guy? Can you make my portrait?" After some time Jingky replied," I am Jingky from the Philippines. Thank you so much for your appreciation Mam. This guy is from Gujarat. Yes I can make a portrait of yours." They started chatting in this way.

Susmita wrote," I will wait for my portrait. I am a widow and a school teacher. I have my only son and mom in law in my family. What about you?"

Jingky replied," Yes mam I will certainly do your portrait. I have four siblings. I am an adopted child of my parents. I work in the Philippine embassy."

Susmita wanted to know eagerly how she knew Meva? But she was hesitating to ask her this question directly. So she asked her," Have you ever come to India ? Is he your relative? Can you make such a beautiful portrait of mine like him?"

" No mam, I didn't come to India. But in the future I have plans to come . This guy is not my relative. I met him through an app. He is Sameer. He wanted my Instagram Id and we started following each other. Yes mam I will make yours like him." She replied.

" From how many days have you known him? You wrote so beautiful lines on him. I also write stories , poetries if you want I can share them with you". Susmita wrote.

Jingky replied," Oh ! Sure mam, I would love to read your writing. I have known him for the last two months. And frankly speaking we fell in love with each other. Though you can say it's too early to love someone for a little time.I don't know but Sameer just touched my heart. I told my mom about him. My mom was also surprised. You know I feel very happy to talk to him."

" Oh! That is. Okay bye bye. Nice to talk to you. Stay good". Writing this Susmita stopped chatting with her.

Susmita felt so jealous of her. Her anger went to her more than Sameer. Meva was only hers. No one could get him. She decided in her mind that she would never let the relationship happen between them. A few days earlier she wanted someone to come in his life so that he could be very happy. After knowing from Jingky she felt her heart was empty as if something precious had stolen from her. She didn't sleep well the whole night. She was thinking about how to destroy their love.

So in the early morning Susmita wrote to Jingky," Hey Jingky! Good morning. I think I know this guy very well. His nick name is Meva. Which means sweets.He is from Umbergaon. He has his parents,one elder sister and one younger brother. Am I right?" She also wrote his mobile number.

Jingky replied," How do you know so much about him ? Do you know him? Please tell me mam. It's very important to me. Is he married! I am done with him."

Susmita said,"Ask him , who is Susmita? He will tell you.I Have nothing more to tell you. Ta ta. Have a great day". Writing it she stopped chatting.

In the evening Sameer unblocked her from Instagram and messaged her," What the hell have you said to Jingky? She was crying. Tell her you lied.You always said me to find someone and now you are trying to fucked up my life"? Why?"

Susmita replied," I also cried the whole day .Only for you I betrayed my husband. I told you I wanted you as my little friend , you wanted me as your girlfriend. Now regret is left in my life."

"What happened, just forget. I love Jingky. You told me if I get someone you will leave me.I hope you should keep your words. Don't ruin my life Susmita.I request you.Sameer wrote.

Susmita cried a lot that night. She didn't take her meal. Then Ashish was at home. He and Nipa thought she was crying for Arijit. Sometimes she tears while standing in front of Arijit's photo. Susmita loved Sameer so much. She didn't deny his request.

The next day she wrote to Jingky," Please don't leave Meva. He never loved me. How could he love me! We have such a big age difference! It was me who loved him . It was one sided love. I made my husband fool only for him. Meva had no fault.Actually I was obsessed with him. It was all my fault. Please don't mind. He is a very good guy. And he loves you very much. "

From that day Susmita tried to forget her Meva. She understood that Sameer was losing interest in her. Falling in love was easy but forgetting someone who once loved madly was very tough. Susmita felt so depressed that she didn't even feel anything good about writing . The small silly things which they did during those four years all started to come to her mind.She didn't have much experience of teenage love or love after marriage. She felt real love with Sameer. People can say it was an insanity of her heart. She really became crazy after getting Sameer in her life. She cried everyday in front of God and prayed to Him to give her peace.

One day Sameer texted her on Instagram," Hey Sus! How are you? Did you forget me? Please forgive me. And blocked Jingky. I love you more than her, you know it. Don't keep any relation with her".

" Meva, I thought to myself to make you free from everything. I don't want to spoil your life". Susmita replied.

Though she knew it was hard for her. She deeply loved him. Before Jingky, she knew Meva also loved her very much. She blocked Jingky at Meva's instruction without any reason. Love is a passion.Love makes people mad. So she also became crazy about Sameer's love.So she couldn't deny his order. She still thought he was careful of her. It made Susmita very happy.

Time went by, Susmita got little popularity as an author. Her simple language and good narration in her book was loved by people. Her first book was published in Sameer's name. Slowly she discovered her Meva obsession was decreasing. Sameer always blocked her if he got angry. And most of the time Susmita had to make him cool by requesting again and again. That made her bored with Sameer. His love with Jinky made Susmita more upset with

Sameer. But they. chatted sometimes.

One day Susmita unblocked Jingky and sent her the link to her book. So that she could read it from abroad. Susmita needed to promote her book. Then Sameer texted her," Why did you send her link? She is not interested in it?" Susmita understood he was keeping relations with both of her as well as Jingky. So she stopped talking to him and tried to make her free from this insanity.

After a few days Sameer went to Budapest for office work. Sameer did not tell her anything about it. He was hiding everything from her. He didn't tell her about her elder sister's marriage ceremony. Before that he told every little thing to Susmita As if Susmita became an enemy to him.

She didn't know he had gone to Budapest. So she texted him to see his post in Budapest. "How are you Meva? Where are you?"Are You in the Philippines! To meet Jingky?

Sameer replied," I am in Budapest.You stopped talking to me. So I couldn't tell you. I missed you a lot. Please talk to me for some time. It's too cold here. 9 degrees Celsius . I am alone here."

" What about Jingky? Congratulations on your journey. You love her so talk to her.You hate me .You always block me but you don't block her. You only used me.Day after day you provoked me to fall in your love. I didn't listen to my brain, I only followed my heart .I am so stupid that I have to hide you secretly in my mind. I can't say anything about you to anyone. First, people will not believe it all, secondly they will not blame you. As I am a woman and older than you. All will tell me about a characterless woman. What did I do tell me? Only I love you madly.Trust you blindly. Thought you as my God. Give you priority over everything. This is my fault! You never value me as you know Susmita is an idiot. Saying all Susmita stopped.

CHAPTER TWENTY-ONE

THE TOUCH OF BREEZE

THE TOUCH OF BREEZE (PART-21)

" Sus!Please keep quiet! Don't say that. I also love you. There is no lie in it. God knows how much I love you. But you don't want me Jaan. And frankly speaking I don't have that courage to go against everything. " Sameer replied.

You know I am not as clever as Jingky. Today I am telling you. How much I love you no one can ever love you so much. I published my first book with your name. How much love is behind it!When you will understand then it will be late." By writing all her eyes filled with tears.

"Please cool down. We both didn't do anything wrong. We fell in love with each other.We didn't understand that reality is tough.I am not talking to Jingky. I love you more than anything.So I get angry with you easily. I know if there is someone who always will support me, that is you. So I block you. I love when you try to make me cool by sending texts to me again and again. make Sus, my babe please talk to me. I want to hear your voice. Can I call you over the phone?" Sameer wrote.

That day Susmita and Sameer talked to each other for an hour.Sameer said, " Thank you so much Jaan. For talking to me. Please kiss me my love. I am hungry for it. Susmita, please tell me, do you really love me? If I hurt you someday will you forgive me? Sus,you may be right. There is no happy ending to our love story. We fell in love with each other only to hurt us. I want you from the heart but I know I can't do this. I am the eldest son of my parents.

I have lots of responsibilities. I said I don't care about anything but really I am a coward. My dad promised his friend that I should marry his daughter. I will never forget you. Your two beautiful eyes and your sweet smile will always remain the same in my heart. I will keep hidden our love in my soul forever. I wanted you to hate me and throw me out of your life. So that I don't get hurt by thinking that you became an unfaithful woman, only for me. I don't know if I can ever make a happy family with someone. You are my wife. You have full right on me, my love.I want to come to Kolkata to see you Sus!

Susmita said," Sameer today I am telling you if I really love someone from the heart that is you. I know my love story is rare. It may not have a happy ending. I loved Arijit also. But due to the pressure of reality that love was destroyed. There was only responsibility left in between us.There were a few drops of love at the end but it was not so thrilling. We both were tired of our relationship. We didn't break up only for Ashish. After loving you I realized the meaning of love. I forgot my age and my boundaries. I became younger in front of you. I became angry with you , cried for you. If I didn't know your news I would be so anxious. Maybe we got married online but for me you are my husband. In reality our marriage has no value.The day will always be memorable for me. The feeling of that day never will die from my mind. Meva I wanted to make you free from all the boundaries. Get married with your dad's choice and live happily. Only keep in mind there is a Bengali woman, far from you but loves you unconditionally. Pray for you everyday. Put Sindoor on your name so that you get a long life. I never got a beautiful married life. But I am grateful to my husband because he married me when I was nothing. I got Ashish with him.That is a pride for me. When you came to my life then I thought of you as my little friend. But slowly I started loving you. I forgot everything , my limitations. People say go to your heart. I followed that and hurt myself and cheated both of my husband and you. I am sorry for everything. Only one request: I want to see my name again on your beautiful hairy chest. Before my death I want to see you once. Please make a promise. This is my last request. I will wait for you. You are not my love for this life. We will meet in another life. "

Sameer said ," What are you saying like nonsense. I don't believe in the next life. If there is true love in between us we will meet in this life. I also want my name on your breast. I promise I will certainly meet you in this birth. You don't need to wait for the next birth. We will bury our love into our heart. I love you Sus. Sameer told.

" What happened to Jingky? Meva, Don't you love her? Are you broke up?" She asked

" I don't know what happened to her.Now a days we don't talk.Why are you asking all? When your husband was alive you fell in my love ? Don't you? Then I never asked you anything about him. Susmita ,we are human beings. We follow some rules of life to make life peaceful. Otherwise our mind is wild. I know you always feel guilty about our love. I fall for Jingky but I love you more than her. Just keep it in mind that the feelings that I have for you will never die." Sameer wrote.

She realized Jingky and Sameer had some problems. She felt very happy thinking about it. Only for her once Meva, talked to her badly. Susmita saw how Arijit behaved with her rudely so she didn't like it.

Only to make Jingky jealous she texted her by unblocking her Instagram account." Hey Jingky, how are you? How is my Meva? Now he is in Budapest. After coming here he will come to meet me. Will you do me a favor please! Tell him that I had bought a marker to write his name on my breast. He wanted to see it. And you know he is my God. So I have to fulfill all his wishes. He said he will also write my name on his chest. I felt shy to tell him. So I request you to tell him everything. Stay happy ." Then she again blocked Jingky so that she could not reply to her.

Within a few times Sameer texted her on WhatsApp ," Why did you say everything to her? She is going to be my family. I am serious about it. I will marry her. Our two families agreed about it. Susmita what do you want? Hun! Tell me. I can't appreciate your actions. If you do anything anymore I will have to take strong action against you." He wrote more messages. Without seeing anything Susmita deleted it all. She didn't reply.

Then Sameer called her continuously over the phone. She received the call and said while crying,"Meva you threatened only for her? Like my husband. I am afraid of you like Arijit. Arijit always made her afraid.(by saying, 'do you want to see my real form?') All men are the same. From today I don't need any man in my life. You were playing with me? Listen, today I am telling you. If you make me cry today then one day you have to cry for me also. From today there is no Sameer in Susmita's life.I am going to block you forever. You are free. I don't need your love or your insult. I made the mistake of running after you. I don't know if I will ever forgive myself." Then she blocked him from WhatsApp.

Throughout the whole day Sameer called her again and again but Susmita didn't receive his call. She promised to herself to stop everything. This was the first time she blocked him. Her tears came, her heart was bleeding but she made herself hard . She let her Meva live freely. This time Sameer didn't block her. Sameer changed the profile with this line," Let's Universe decide". Susmita realized that it was written about her. Their love story ended. Everything which has started must have an end. There was an unknown attraction of love which still didn't get them apart. After that she didn't keep any contact with him. Even she deleted his number. Whenever she sees the name of Sameer anywhere or gets the touch of breeze her soul takes her to their beautiful incomplete love story. She made herself busy with writing. She set a goal to become a good story writer. Slowly how much she proved herself as a good writer her Meva erased from her mind that much. Only memories left.

She didn't understand what happened to her then! As a serious teacher, how could she love a man so much she didn't know the answer. The readers of this story will find out many explanations. Maybe she didn't get Arijit properly. Or maybe she didn't love anyone ever or it was her obsession. Or maybe she didn't love herself.

Whatever it was that love brought a fresh touch of breeze in her boring life. That love made herself a good author. People say fallout in love makes someone a poet or can be demolished. She became a good writer.

Writing everything she shut down her laptop. Her heart became heavy. Her eyes got wet. Now She forgot Meva's phone number. His beautiful face remained the same in her heart as earlier. She wanted to know how Meva is now? She imagined that he had a beautiful wife and a happy family with children. So many days she suppressed Meva into her heart not to memorize him. But after writing everything she felt her heart become light. Her Meva had been lost from her life but the love of Breeze will never die from her heart.

It was almost evening. She needed a cup of tea to refresh her. So she called the hotel boy. They gave her snacks and tea. While taking tea she called Shilpa.

She said, "Oh! Granny , are you okay? Have you finished your writing? After coming back I will read it first. Now we are in Bhojbasa. There are other peoples who are also staying here. Tonight we will stay here . Tomorrow early morning we will start for Goumukh and Tapovan. You know here the people are very cautious about environmental pollution. There was no plastic on the entire road. You just can't imagine being so neat and clean! When we first reached the Gangotri forest check post. They checked our pass and you know they counted our plastic bottles and bags. And told us to bring every counted plastic otherwise we have to give a penalty.We had to submit a caution money. Granny !I saw a cute little hilly bird in the forest. I captured it in my camera. I saw a crow with a yellow beak. While we were walking on the hilly road the river Bhagarathi was flowing with us. We walked almost 4 km and reached Deogarh. There we drank the pure water from the fall. All said it was like mineral water. We were so tired that we stayed there for half an hour and had our breakfast. Then we started walking again. You know Granny , it was an adventure. Most of all felt the breathing problem but people were walking tirelessly. How strange it is! I was thinking that we all were like addicts. Then we reached Bhalubasa. We rested there for some time. From there Chirbasa was only 2 km. There is a mountain called Hanumanpit. You know Granny ,there was an old man about seventy years old walking beside me. I was amazed to see him. I called him Dadai. He came here three times. I captured everything in my camera. Let me come, I will show you everything . Then I missed you a lot. You could easily come if you want. There was a tree whose name was Bhojpatra tree.Do you know why it is popular ? " Saying everything, Shilpa stopped for a while.

" Yes I know why the tree is so famous? Maharshi Balmiki wrote the Indian epic Ramayana on the bark of this tree. This tree can only be found in the Himalaya mountain. Am I right, sweety? Now tell me, do you know the story of Ramayana? Listen, I am good. Tell me more about your experience. I may not have gone with you but I can imagine by hearing your description. That I am with you. You know I am a writer. So my imagination is more powerful than others." Susmita said with a laugh .

" I know my Granny knows everything. I am sorry I don't know the story of Ramayana. Later I want to hear from you. You know there was a small wooden pool over the river. Mom was very afraid to walk over it. I was also afraid. Dad told us to cross carefully. Then we reached Chirbasa. It was 3571 m high. There we saw some small plants named Ganga tulsi. People say the leaves of the plants give a supply of oxygen. So we smelled the leaves. I got a light smell of Basil leaves. I don't know if it really supplies oxygen or not. But I am surprised to see the creation of nature. There were lots of falls and everyone collected drinking water from them. There were lots of big and small stones spreaded. It was like a desert of stones. The government had done a good job. After a few miles there were milestones where the name and the description of place were written. So that the tourists get a concept of their trekking. Then we reached Bhojbasa after four hours . There are lots of hotels for the tourists. And it was not so costly. They provide fooding and logging both. In the afternoon the peaks were looking so beautiful with light sunlight I can't say you in words. On the other hand, some people were doing videos for you tube channels. I was astonished to see people's enthusiasm. We took our lunch here. We all are praying for good weather so that we can finish the rest of the trekking in a good way." Saying all she stopped.

CHAPTER TWENTY-TWO

THE TOUCH OF BREEZE

THE TOUCH OF BREEZE(PART-22)

Then she said," Granny, I will call you tomorrow. Now talk to mom and dad". She handed the phone to Ashish.

Susmita talked to Ashish and Rina for some time. Her heart felt light! She was feeling cold. So she didn't want to go to the hall for dinner. She opened her laptop for writing. She was thinking she never waited for Sameer. She didn't know someone like Sameer could come to her life ever. When he came to her life she didn't realize it was him because Sameer was not her goal or dream or hope ever. Sameer was a surprise, a cyclone, a gift and an adventure in her life. He was the beginning of a story .Which she never imagined that something like could happen. She wanted to be happy with Arijit like other common Bengali women. When she understood it would never happen then she accepted everything as her luck.Susmita and Sameer loved each other very much and it ended sadly. She wrote that our life is costly and the most valuable thing is love. She realized it for the first time after losing Arijit. We feel our real love when we lose someone. At a certain part of life when she felt it was tough not to talk with her Meva, or not to see him then she needed not to love him. Stupid Susmita did that. She loved him madly. Arijit and Sameer seemed to have gone from her life but the reality was they were very much present in her life.She didn't let them go. Susmita nourished them in her soul carefully. She got touch of Arijit and Sameer's touch was her imagination. If we explain scientifically we can find that our frontal lobe of the brain conducts our reality and our thalamus controls our imagination. In Susmita's case both worked equally. In her whole life she cried for both of them and she sank into both of their love. So when she tried to write a real story her own story came out.

Foolish Susmita wanted love for her whole life but she didn't know what it actually was. She never would meet Arijit again . She tried to search for Arijit in Ashish. Whenever she saw some equality in between them she thought Arijit was there in Ashish. It gave her peace of mind. She wanted to meet Sameer but didn't try. Her Meva is doing well and that thought gave her peace.

After blocking him on WhatsApp she got a call from him after one month. That day her phone rang continuously. That day Nipa fell down in the bathroom. She got a head injury. Susmita took her to the hospital alone. Ashish was then in Mumbai with his wife Rina. Whole of the day she was tense with Nipa. That time after coming home no one was there to talk to her except Nipa. She was then her only companion. Susmita couldn't live alone. So she took great care of her. In the visiting hours her in-laws and relatives came to visit Nipa. She was so tired the whole day that after coming home she just switched off the phone and fell asleep. There was a number in her missed call list for many times that was Sameer's number. She wanted to talk to him but she didn't call him back. Sometimes our mind wants to do something but our brain stops us. Susmita always follows her mind but that time she went to her brain. So she wasn't able to know why Sameer called her.

After two days Nipa came home. That time she needed a care giving person for Nipa . Because Susmita had to go to school. Then she appointed a girl to look after her. Her name was Namita. She was very needy. Later she became a big part of Susmita's life. After her birth her mom died. Her dad got married again. Her step mom didn't like her a little. She forced her to do all the work for the family. Namita did not like to stay there. Her dad looked for a boy for her. Her dad and step mom got her married to her at a young age. She thought she would get relief from this family and step mom. Her husband was a hard worker but a drunk person.

Whenever he drank alcohol he forgot everything. So very often he beat Namita .She didn't want to sleep with him. She came back to her parents.Her parents made her understand to adjust with him. So she again went back to him.But couldn't tolerate his torcher. She decided not to go back and become self sufficient.She passed class ten.Then she started working as a helping hand. She got a job in Susmita's house. With the great care of Namita and with her own wish Nipa got well within one month. Namita was a very kind hearted lady. She took all the responsibility of Nipa and their family. Susmita and Nipa both loved her very much. When Nipa got well Susmita thought of leaving Namita as her salary was too high.But Namita told her," Please Didi don't leave me. Let me work at your home. I have no objection to whatever you pay me. Only I want to stay with you. You know I have no one so think of me as your little sister." Within a few days she became Susmita's friend. After coming home she felt very happy to talk to her. Namita became a part of her family. Every night she went back home after eating dinner. Sometimes she wanted to stay at Susmita's house. Susmita didn't oppose. And then she started staying at Susmita's house. One day she told Susmita," Didi, I love you very much. Did you know Didi why my husband beat me? I didn't love him. I don't like men. I love women. When I slept with him I hated his body. He wanted to love me but I didn't let him. He got angry with me and forced me. Didi, I fell in love with you. Whenever I see you I imagine you as my own." Saying all she laughed.

" What are you saying? Are you crazy? You are insane. You say what comes to your mouth." Susmita scolded her

" No ,Didi, I know what I am saying. I will never leave you. You may not know I loved Indrani .She was one of my schoolmates. We both loved each other. Her dad was rich. We promised not to leave each other ever. We both kissed each other. When I caught her hand I felt so happy.She was very good at studying. She also didn't like boys. She was like me. We did everything together. One day I told her my dad chose a boy for me. That time my dad was trying to get me married. When she heard it she hugged me and cried. She told me," I love you Namita. Please don't get married. We will get married in a few years." Hearing it I told her," What are you saying? How can two girls get married? No one will listen to us. Don't say anything about anyone." Later I understood I love her. After marriage my study stopped and I went to my husband's house. I invited her to my wedding. She came and told my ear, 'Namita I know you love me. You will not stay with your husband. If you feel any problem, come to me. I will wait for you.' Didi, I don't know where she is now. After coming back from my husband's house I knew she had gone to another city for her studies. Now I cry for her. I want her". Her tears came while saying everything.

Susmita understood her pain. What is love she felt from her vanes. She only said," See Namita, there are lots of things happening in the world where we can't do anything. We can't control everything. Time heals something but sometimes not. True love is really painful. If I can do anything for you then I will certainly try to meet your love Indrani, with you."

She worked at Susmita's house for about ten years. In those years she became a family member. She knew lots of things about Susmita's life. Once Susmita was forced to tell her something about Sameer. Susmita opened a bank account for her. There she deposited her salary every month. Sometimes Susmita gave her money as a gift for her good work except of salary. Nipa loved Namita very much like her own daughter.Susmita was very much dependent on Namita about family matters.Susmita took her everywhere like her friend. Ashish called Namita Masi. (Masi means aunt). In Ashish marriage she did everything like his own aunt. The next Durga puja, Ashish gave Namita a smartphone as a gift and taught her how to use it.

She very often talked about Indrani. So One day Susmita opened her Facebook account and said to her," Listen, you can find out your Indrani from here. So try it." Then she taught her how to search. Namita said with Surprise, "Really Didi! Is that possible?" One day after came back from school she found Namita very happy. She asked her the reason. Namita told her," Didi, I got my Indrani from

Facebook. Now she is in Gujrat .We talked over the phone. Now she works in an IT company. She lives alone there. She didn't forget me. She also tried to contact me. But I didn't have a smartphone. I told her everything about me. She said to go to her. Shall I go there? I love her more than anything. What you did for me I will always keep in my mind. I am very much grateful to you for it. I want Indrani's love. We are for each other. I will do something there. Throughout these years I saved a lot of money. I cook well. If I don't get any job then I will start a business of home delivery food supply. I talked to Indrani. She said it will go better there. Please Didi let me go."

Susmita wanted from the heart Namita and Indrani to have a beautiful life together. She didn't think it really could ever happen. She asked her with a smile,"You told me you will never leave me? You love me! What will happen then?"

" Yes Didi , I love you. But you are my Arijit. Indrani is my Sameer. Without her touch my life is incomplete." Susmita couldn't stop her. She talked to Indrani. Knew the address from her. Then she bought a ticket for Namita.She arranged everything for her going to Indrani. She took her to the airport and sent her by flight. Before going Namita hugged Susmita and said with tears," Didi, I am grateful to you. I don't know I will never pay your debt.I want to do something special for you someday."

After reaching Kutch in Gujarat Namita called her. Gave her the news of their togetherness. Susmita's heart was satisfied with it.

CHAPTER TWENTY-THREE

THE TOUCH OF BREEZE

THE TOUCH OF BREEZE (PART-23)

Though Nipa didn't want it. She thought that Namita got a better job. She told her again and again," Namita, don't leave us. What do you need? More salary. I will tell Susmita to give you more. Without you how my life will go."

After Namita's gone Susmita's house became empty. After searching many times she didn't get such a faithful and responsible person for her family. She called Susmita over the phone often and also talked to Nipa.Then Nipa got sick after a few days.She had a very strong mentality. She never bothered anyone for her. Even after her husband's death she handled her family and her sick son. But at the end of her life of two years she got bedridden. She stopped eating. Then doctor gave her rice tube for feeding her. She was in this condition for two years. Susmita did all the responsibilities for her. Before death she blessed Susmita. That was a peace in her life. Throughout her life Susmita loved Nipa like her mom. She never thought that Nipa was her mom in law. Nipa's daughter was far from her. So she always thought Susmita was like her own daughter. Without Susmita's opinion Nipa never wanted to do anything. She never took her meal without Susmita. Before going to school she often said," Susmita take your tiffin in time. Don't forget. Don't do so much hard work. Women need to take care of their health. But we don't care and in the end we suffer." Whenever Susmita thought about Nipa her heart became heavy.

Namita also didn't forget her. Before coming to Haridwar she called Susmita over the phone and Susmita told her everything about her trip.

Her dinner was served in the room. After dinner she opened her laptop. She started typing again.She tried hard to delete Meva's memory from her brain. She didn't know Nipa could understand her affair with Sameer. After falling in Sameer's love she knew love was like that. No one knew why Nipa fell in love with T. Chakraborty betraying her husband. Only for that reason she lost her husband. Her son always hated her. Maybe that's why she spent a long time in front of God for regret. When Susmita looked at her she felt bad. She always tried to keep her happy. From outside Nipa looked well but from inside she broke into pieces. Susmita never asked her about the relationship between her and T. Chakraborty. So she did not know much about that. She heard that Nipa had a photo of that man. Which Arijit threw away once. She gave her husband's marriage ring to T. Chakraborty. Maybe her love story ended with the man with that ring. After Nipa's death as a writer slowly Susmita's name was going to be famous. Her emptiness filled with writing. Except for school and household work she always sat with her laptop. Many publishers contacted her to write for them. Then a famous Bengali newspaper offered her to write for their subscription. She accepted their offer. So she left her school job. She devoted herself to being a good author. Slowly Sameer became less important in her life. After a few years she forgot his number. Her obsession with Sameer faded slowly. She understood it was her insanity. But every morning she didn't stop to put Sindoor. So that Sameer remained safe without getting hurt. She was feeling tired. So she shut down her laptop and fell asleep.

In the morning she got up a little late. After her phone rang ,it was Namita. She received the call. Namita shouted," Didi, how are you? Are you awake or not? How was your journey till now? I know you love hills. Where are you now ? How is Ashish and everyone? After saying all in a breath she stopped.

Susmita replied with smile," I am well. Yes I just woke up. Till now our tour has been very good. You know I am writing a novel. Last night I wrote late. And almost finished it.Ashish and all are good. How about you and Indrani?"

" Didi, we are very well. My home delivery business is going well. You know I cook veg Bengali dishes and people love it very much. Didi, all happened only for you. You taught me so delicious dishes.I wish I can be present on your book publishing occasion. I want to see my Didi's function. Didi you will wear a blue saree. You look beautiful with this color." Namita said.

" Okay I will wear a blue saree. And keep silent! Don't say I did a lot for you. I didn't do anything. I only helped you a little bit. And it was my duty as your elder sister. You want to be present in my book publishing function. Why didn't you tell me before? I wish it could happen this time. If you come to my function I will be very much honored. Listen, now I have to take tea. Let's talk to you later." Susmita said.

" Okay, Didi ,take your breakfast and tea. Didi let me know I and Indrani both will go to that function. Indrani also loves to read your book. Take care Didi. I will call you later." Saying that she put off the phone.

Then Susmita went to the washroom. Due to the cold she didn't want to go to the dinning hall. She called the reception and ordered for her tea and breakfast in the room.After finishing all she opened her laptop for editing. After a while her phone rang with an unknown number. She received it. Someone humbly said, "Hello mam, good morning. Namaste. I am your publisher Deb Kumer Vidarthy. My assistant contacted you a few months earlier. Then you agreed to write a true love story for us. So I want to know the current update. I know now you are in Gangotri. If you could finish it, then I have a plan."

" Oh Namaste. I almost finished it. Only editing left. I guess I can finish it within two days. Now tell me what is your plan?" Susmita replied.

" Mam, if you finish it then we can organize a book publishing party for you here in Dehradun. My whole team is here for a project. So if you agree then we can approach further. We can fix the date next week. There we will sign the contract paper. So let me know mam. All will be done as you wish." Dev Kumer said.

Susmita thought it would be a good idea.Ashish, Rina and Silpa will be present there. And they all will be very happy. Rina's little aunt lives in Dehradun and they planned to stay there for four days. From there they will take their flight from Jolly Grant Airport Dehradun to Kolkata. She thought not to say anything to Ashish. Because he always loved to surprise others, Susmita would surprise him at the function. Thinking about it Susmita smiles a little.

CHAPTER TWENTY-FOUR

THE TOUCH OF BREEZE

THE TOUCH OF BREEZE(PART-24)

" It's a good idea. We are staying in Dehradun next week. I think you should read the story once. If you don't like then what will happen ?" Susmita said.

" Yeah Mam, you are such a famous writer! How can I not like it.This is my email number. Please send it there. It will be my pleasure. My editor will check it. I know everyone will like it. Then we are going to do the function next week. I will send you every detail of it on your WhatsApp. Okay mam. Bye, take care." Saying that he turned off the phone.

Susmita started reading her novel. She changed where it was necessary.

Silpa called her at noon.And said," Granny! Do You know where we are now? Now we are in Tapovan. Here is an Ashram where we are taking rest.We will start for Gangotri after a while and will reach at night. What are you doing? Writing? Are you well?"

" Wow! You have reached Tapovan.I think you enjoyed it a lot. I am good. Now I am editing. I have finished my writing. Now tell me your trekking experience. I want to get those feelings with my imagination."

" You know Granny, last night we stayed at Bhojbasa. Early this morning we started for Tapovan. At first we sat on a pulley to cross the river. Pulley is like a small box. Everyone had a stick on hand for trekking. Then we started walking. Dad took a guide for Tapovan trekking. On the left side Bhagirathi peak and on the right mount Shivling peak. In between we were walking. Trekking is very tough here. Everywhere was bolder throughout the whole road. We had to take a rest after a few times. Throat was drying.So we took enough water. We were astonished to see Gomukh. Its height is 13200 ft. Such large glaciers! River Ganga is flowing at high speed. Only a howling noise. Luckily we had a power bank. Otherwise we can't talk. Tapovan is on the right side of Goumukh. There were holders all around so an avalanche could happen at any time. Then we started for Tapovan. It's height is 14300 ft. Walking was too tough here. The Roads were very steep. It was only 3 km but as if it was 5 km far. When we reached Tapovan we forgot the pain of trekking. As if we reached heaven. Large open area without boundaries. There were many peaks like mount Meru, on the left side Bhagirati one, two, three peaks. So beautiful! Words are not enough to describe. Weather changes at any time. I took excellent shots. I will upload them all on Youtube. Granny! Do you know why Ganga is called Bhagirati, Jannavi ,Ganga?"

" No, I don't know. Have you heard of it? Then tell me now!" Susmita said with curiosity.

Silpa said," The Babaji of Tapovan Ashram told us the story. Bhagirat's son King Sagar had sixty thousand sons. They did Ashwamedha Yajna. God Indra stole their Yajna horse and hid it in Kapil Rishi's Ashram. When king Sagar ones it he scolded Rishi Kapil and in anger Rishi Kapil killed his sixty thousands sons by burning. And said they would never be free if they don't get the holy Ganga water. So Bhagirat started meditation of Lord Shiva to bring Ganga on the land. When Ganga came to the land she was very huge. For that reason the Ashram of Jannavi Rishi got destroyed. So he stopped Ganga. Bhagirat again prayed for Ganga. Then Jannavi released Ganga and it started flowing. So Ganga is called Bhagirati , Jannavi, Ganga."

" Wow! What a fantastic story. How are mom and dad? When you will come back. I am waiting for you." Susmita said.

" Okay Granny! We have to come down. See you at night. Bye." Saying it she cut the phone.

Susmita sent her story to the publisher's email. At 8 PM Silpa and her parents came back to the hotel. They quickly made them fresh and had dinner. After coming to the room Silpa wanted to read the story. Susmita said," Mithi,you are tired. Read it tomorrow." Granny! You know I go to bed late. It's my habit. I will read it now. Tomorrow early morning we will leave the hotel and start for Derahdun. I wanna be your first reader." Silpa said with a smile.

She started reading. She asked," Granny, who is Sameer? Is he alive or imagination! Wow what a beautiful story. And your imagination is just awesome. I have to finish the whole of it." Susmita felt happy. Silpa finished it around 1 a.m. Susmita fell asleep.

The next day they started for Deradhun at 7 AM. It was a 9 hour journey by car. On the way Silpa said to Rina," You know mom! Granny's story is just superb. You were shouting why didn't I get up early! Did you know I finished it late last night?

" Oh! That is. Then tell the summary of the story." Ashish said.

" The hero is fifteen years older than the heroine. Their love and marriage was online but without happy ending and after twenty years the Bengali heroine put Sindoor on his name for his long and healthy life." Silpa said.

" Wow! Interesting. I guess the heroine is backdated. Now the Bengali women don't put Sindoor. See your mom! Hey Rina do you put Sindoor for me!" Ashish said with laugh.

"Hey, what are you saying? Every married woman tries to put it if she loves her husband. See! I put or not." Saying it she showed her hairline.

" Oh! So small! Need a microscope to see it." While Ashish said it all laughed.

" You know this heroine is a widow and she put Sindoor on the back side of her head. So that no one could see it." Silpa said.

"That means the heroine still loves the hero." Rina said.

CHAPTER TWENTY-FIVE

THE TOUCH OF BREEZE

THE TOUCH OF BREEZE (PART-25)

On the way Susmita said to Ashish," Babu, I have finished my novel. The publisher called me. We are staying at Rina's aunt house for four days in Dehradun. He requested me to organise the book publishing function there in Vasant Biher in Dehradun. There is a big community hall so day after tomorrow, in the evening they want to do it. You people never joined in that function so I agreed. I thought you will be happy. They will send us car to take there.What do you think?"

Before Ashish could say something Silpa shouted in joy. "Hurrah! So many days I thought about seeing my Granny's book publishing function. Really Granny! Please do it here." Ashish said with a smile," Mom! You surprised me! Congratulations. You know Mithi , I always surprise your Granny! So this time your Granny did it to me . I am very happy mom, with your decision. I am proud of you."

Rina also congratulated Susmita and said," Mom, really it is happening here. I know that community hall. It is near my aunt's house. So we all are going."

" They send me every detail in my WhatsApp. Only we have to send your aunt's address. After reaching their home please send it." Susmita said to Rina.

At 10 AM they stopped near a restaurant and had their breakfast. After that Rina, Ashish, Silpa all fell asleep in the car. They were very tired. Susmita was tensed about her novel. Though she knew it was one of her beat novel. She was waiting for the reaction of the publisher.She already texted Namita about the function. If she and Indrani could come. But from Kutch to Dehradun the distance is 1411 km and it takes around 25 hours by train. Susmita was sure Namita wouldn't join. But if they could come it would be great. At that time a message entered her phone from Devkumer email. " Unique story mam. My heartiest congratulations. My team has already decided to promote you. Only after reaching Dehradun let us know. So we are going to meet the day after tomorrow at the community hall. Thank you mam." Susmita felt so pleased. Hearing the appreciation of her own creation.They finished their lunch on the way. Susmita showed Silpa Devkumer's e-mail. Silpa said," See Granny, I told you it is an amazing story."

Almost 4.30 PM they reached Rina's little aunt's house. They all were very tired. Her little aunt Rupa, her husband Dipankar and only daughter Subhra became very glad. Dehradun0 is a beautiful clean city with mild weather. The next day they visited the famous places in Dehradun like Tapokeswar temple, Robber's cave, Malsi deer Park etc. The next day all were thrilled with Susmita's book publishing function. In the evening the car came to take them to the hall. Rupa and her family also went there. Susmita wore a blue saree. She looks perfect in blue. There were lots of people in the audience seat. All sat in their seats. Suddenly Namita came and hugged her. Susmita said in amazement," You have come. How! I thought you can't" Namita replied, " Didi, we didn't want to miss this beautiful moment so we first came to Bhuj by car and from there by flight here . Meet my Indrani". Susmita hugged Indrani and said,'' You take good care of my Namita . So I am grateful to you." Indrani answered," I got her only for you so all credit goes to you Didi."

In the meantime the host called Susmita on the stage. She introduced her to the audience. Susmita said she dedicated her book to her husband Arijit and special thanks to her granddaughter Silpa. The host requested her to tell the summary of the story. After finishing, the audience stood and clapped. Then a fair and tall man about 45 to 50 years old came to the stage and kneel down before her. Then he gave her a rose and said,"Sus, I love you my Jaan ''. Susmita was astonished! She became speechless. He is Meva! Her Sameer. Sameer took the microphone and said," I am Sameer. Susmita's secret love. Twenty years ago I didn't have that courage to catch her hand. Today I am telling you I love her and I will love her till my end." Susmita tried to stop him by saying," What are you doing, Meva? Please stop". He said," Sus! Please let me say to them, " Time fades everything but my love Susmita didn't go far from me a little during this long time. We never touched each other.I feel her every moment. Our online marriage has no value in front of others. The insanity of that evening never erased from my heart. I called her many times , and I wanted to meet her. She became famous. I thought she hated me and she forgot about me. I read Susmita's book.I got married after my dad's wish but it broke up. Then I came to Kutch. When Namita told me Susmita loves me till now , I didn't believe it. Namita, Dev please come here." All the spectators were amazed. Essentially Silpa. She didn't understand. Susmita couldn't believe her eyes. Namita said, " While working at Didi's home one day I saw her putting on Sindoor. Didi didn't want to tell me. I forced her then she said Sameer.I told her Didi, you don't live together. You don't have any relationship then why do you put Sindoor?" She said,' I promised him. We may not live together, that doesn't mean our love was a lie. I am bearing his love in my soul till now. Then she told me hey, don't tell anyone about it. Sameer is my imagination. Writers are like that. I realized Didi loves Sameer very much. So I thought of doing something for her. I wanted to pay my debt. I started searching for Sameer Dhuker from Facebook. I sent friend requests to them and chatted with them. Al last I got one from Kutch. While chatting I told Didi's name and he started quarring me. I was doubtful. So I and Indrani met him. I told him everything about Didi. Sameer said " She hates me . On the last day I did something wrong with her. After knowing about our relationship Jingky broke up with me but we were Instagram friends. My dad threatened me that if I don't marry his friend's daughter then he will kill himself. So I didn't have any options. That day Jingky sent me the screenshot of Susmita's text and said with fun,' See your Insane girlfriend! She is just mad for you. She has bought a marker to write your name on her breast." Then I lied to Susmita that I am going to marry Jingky and she is going to be my family. So that Susmita would erase me from her life'. I made him understand that Didi really loves him like before. To make sure he took the help of Devkumer." Devkumer said," I am a publisher. Sameer is my close friend. When I knew about it I made a plan. I needed a good love story. I gave her a proposal to write a true story for me.She agreed. In fact Sameer talked to her as my assistant that day and told her what to write. Sameer said to me if she writes about him then he will believe that she loves him.``

Namita continued," There is another one who helped a lot to make the plan successful. Without him nothing will be possible. He is our Ashish and Rina gave him full support. Didi is lucky to have a son like him. When I told him everything about Didi and Sameer he said,' Aunty, all of her life my mom only served others. If they both love each other truly then I will do my best to make them together.' Then everything was going according to the plan. There was only one doubt if Didi can't finish her writing within the time. Then we thought of doing the function in Mumbai on Diwali. That was our second plan."

Ashish came on the stage and took Susmita's hand and gave to Sameer's hand and said," From today you live your life as you desire. We are always beside you." Then he looks at Susmita and says with a loud laugh,"How is my surprise ,mom!" All were clapping. Silpa came and hugged her dad and said," I am proud of my dad". Susmita's eyes were filled with tears. It was not for sorrow but for happiness.

www.ingramcontent.com/pod-product-compliance
Lightning Source LLC
Chambersburg PA
CBHW031137130726
47988CB00006B/2419